Dancing
ON THE
Edge
OF
Ecstasy

Dancing
ON THE
Edge
OF
Ecstasy

A journey to find true love

Cara Carón

XULON PRESS

Xulon Press
2301 Lucien Way #415
Maitland, FL 32751
407.339.4217
www.xulonpress.com

Printed in the United States of America.

Paperback ISBN-13: 978-1-6628-1298-9
Ebook ISBN-13: 978-1-66281-299-6

ACKNOWLEDGEMENTS

To all those souls
that paint the
Rainbow Colors
On the canvas
of my life

One can be the master of what ones does,
but never of what one feels
…Gustave Flaubert

TABLE OF CONTENTS

Chapter 1

MEMORIES OF SHAWANO

Sitting in my comfy wing chair and looking out at the dazzling, white fluffy banks of snow here in Connecticut, I felt at peace. My life was whirling through my mind. Mom always looked at the glass as full. Everything was good or would be alright in the end. I am thinking how it was for me. Even thought she had such a beautiful philosophy, she always seemed sad and close to tears. I hoped one day she would be happy.

I was five. We had just moved to Shawano Wisconsin. It was a blustery, chill, day and I could barely see out of the window through the frost. I tried to quickly run my hand around the window in a circle and hope it would not stick. We moved here from Milwaukee. Dad got a new job at the cement company. I was bored. I was trying to figure out what to do with myself. My brother, Carl was two. He always wanted me to play with him.

Mother would sit me on a chair, in the middle of the living room and cut my sandy brown hair with her sewing scissor. I could not sit still. I looked like Buster Brown. Mom always called me Molly; my given name was Marie. Dad always called me Molly Poots. If my mother were upset with me, she would call me Marie Catherine.

We played upstairs on the second floor, in a bedroom, and it had a crystal doorknob. The doorknob was loose, and it had no backside to it. We used the doorknob to open the door, but it would fall out. My brother and I were inside. I had to put my finger through a hole in the door where the doorknob should have been, to open the door for Carl.

This house was in the middle of a furrowed, farm field. No one had been living in it for some time until we came. It had no electric lights, no indoor plumbing. At night we would have an indoor pot. No other heat than a potbelly stove. We used kerosene lamps. Rent was six dollars a month.

Thanksgiving, my grandparents came from Milwaukee. We were having dinner, at the table, a huge buck jumped up on the ledge of the bay window and back off, without breaking the window. We all held our breath. Friday grandpa and grandma had to go back to Milwaukee. I was sad to see them go.

One day trauma hit. We had a round table with a purple satin tablecloth on it, with a long gold fringe. My little brother was running around the living room, he pulled on the fringe and the kerosene lamp flew, broke in pieces and the glass gashed his forehead. No phone, my mother put the little guy in the buggy and ran way up the road, to the top of the hill, to the old maid's house. They had a phone. My dad came and they did get Carl to the doctor and got some stitches and he ended up with a big bandage above his brow.

Our house had no running water. We had to go outdoors and pump the water from the well and bring it in to use in the pail with a dipper for drinking. Mom asked me to go out to the pump and bring in some water. I had to prime the pump by putting some water in at the top. I had to hang on the handle, with both hands. I filled the pail only half full so I could carry it by the handle. I took a few steps, put it down, another few steps and put it down until I got to the house. I was out of breath. Wanting to help my mother, I would do anything to make her happy.

The only way to take a bath per se was for mom to heat water on top of the wood burner. We had to pour it into a huge, oval, copper wash tub. Mom would put both of us in it on the living room floor. She waited until the water was cooler so we would not get burned.

On a summer day my grandfather, my dad's father, came to the farm. It was time to slaughter the pig. How they killed it, I will never know. I did hear a bang from the house. I came out. They had hung it up with a big rope and slit it all the way down its stomach and it bled. I put both hands over my eyes. I got sick to my stomach. My mother came to be with me. I was not meant to live on a farm. She took me to the house to calm me.

Monday, Mom said that dad was supposed to kill a chicken for dinner. She forgot to tell him. I wanted to help. I went into my dad's bedroom and next to the bed on the floor were lying his old dirty blue jeans. I knew he carried a pocketknife. I reached in one of his pockets and luckily his knife was there. I took it and could barely open the knife. I went to the chicken coop. I chased the chickens around until I grabbed one and I started to cut back and forth on its neck. The neck just would not come off. I could barely hold on to the chicken. It kept flapping its wings. My mother came out and found me.

"What in the world are you doing? I just looked down. It will be all right." She locked the ailing chicken in the coop until my father got home.

We had pigs at the barn, and they used to try to nuzzle under the wire fence with their little snouts and get out. I was frightened that they would run away so I would not come up for lunch. My mother would cut up a hot dog on a plate for me to eat. I would sit cross-legged on the ground at the fence until my father came home. When he came home, he picked me up in his arms.

"The pigs will not run off the face of the earth." I began to choke up. He always raised his voice, but we were never allowed to cry in front of him. Just another day on the farm.

Chapter 2

FIRST DAY OF SCHOOL

$\mathcal{M}$y parents and I had to go see Miss Haas, the schoolteacher. Mom put on my dress, combed my hair. We needed to get registered. Spring came and the first day of school, I wore the dress that my grandmother had sewed from printed flour sacks. They came from some of my father's, sisters' farms. Flour sacks had tiny floral patterns all over of bright colors, so people could recycle them.

Miss Haas was the only teacher for all eight grades. The one school in the area was a one room schoolhouse. It was supposed to be white, but the paint was peeling. At the top was a large bell that Miss Haas would ring when recess was over. Inside was a creaky old wood floor that made noise every time you took a step.

My cousins and I all went to the same school. I was the only kindergartner. I had to go up front and read with the first and the second grader. All three of us would memorize Robert Louis Stevenson.

In the morning, I told Miss Haas, with her dark brown hair, pulled back with a pug behind her head and a white, long sleeve blouse with a black pleated skirt and black lace up shoes, that I had to go to the bathroom. The bathroom at the school was an outhouse. The wood, creaky floor was on a slant going east in other words downward.

Miss Haas said, " You just got here, go sit down." I let it go and it trickled down the aisle to her desk. My cousin was in eighth grade and he was embarrassed. I could not wait for my mother and brother to take me home. Glad it was Friday. Our dog ran to me. He was a black-and-white spaniel called Schnappsie. We got him from my uncle who had two other dogs named Brandy and Beer.

On Saturday, the horse got out of the barn and was running down the field. It was a parade. First the horse, then my mother, and then the goat and finally the dog. I stood petrified at the house, covering my eyes as I did when I was scared. I almost wet my pants. It all worked, and the horse got back in the barn. My father took care of that.

In the Fall, my kitty Snowball was out in the tall field, when the farmer cut the wheat. She was so little she could not be seen and when we found her, her legs had been sheared off. I had a little burial ceremony in the backyard and laid both hands over the mound of dirt. I prayed she would go to animal heaven. I still had my little tiger cat, until he ate the rat poisoning in the basement. It was a lot for a little girl to process. My father always insisted I be strong and carry on. I could never cry if he were watching. A lump would be in my throat, never let the tears flow while dad was there.

On Wednesday, my parents were going to town and would not be home when I would get out of school. They told me that I should just walk home. At the end of our long, long driveway, we had tied my cousin's goat to a post. My parents could not understand my fright about walking home after school. They put a stick at the end of the driveway for me. They told me that I would be fine. I was still scared after school.

I went with my schoolmates, Pauline and her brother toward where I thought my grandmother might live, some distance, the opposite direction of my house. I loved my paternal grandma. Every time she would see you, she would pinch your cheek and say, "My little Toodledum."

My parents were coming home with the new wash tub on the top of the old model A coupe belonging to my grandfather. They saw me coming down the road, stopped and I was swatted for not listening to directions. I was always afraid and always wanted to make things better. I was an extremely nervous child and bit my nails down to skin. I wet my bed every night.

It was Monday, my mother always washed clothes on Monday. The washing machine was wooden. It had wooden slats with a band of metal around it to hold the slats together. It had a large wooden wheel with a wooden handle. To swish the clothes around you had to move the handle back and forth. The ringer was attached to the machine. It had two rubber rollers and a handle. Put the piece of clothing between the two rubber rollers and then turn the handle to make it go through to take out the water. We had a washboard if something had a stain. I would hand the clothespins to my mom as she hung the clothes on the line.

Mom told me that today was my parents' anniversary. When my mother went into the house, I asked for a scissor to work with my paper dolls. I ran down the long driveway and picked some pink wild roses that were along the road. I cut them with my scissors. The thorns pricked my finger. I ran and gave them to my mother. She hugged me.

Chapter 3

ACCIDENT REVEALED

*I*t was September, I was looking down the driveway and saw a man in his old, red, rusty pickup truck. Mom came out. The man got out of his truck and he told my mom that my father was hurt.

"What happened?"

"Your husband is in Shawano Hospital. He fell twenty-six feet to the pavement while holding guide wires for a house his company was moving.

"Is he alive?"

"Yes, he is alive, you need to come with me to go to the hospital."

Mom was nervous and had trouble catching her breath. She took my brother and I with her. My mother did not drive. Once we got to the hospital, she knew he would be there for quite some time, but he would live.

My mother knew we would have to do something different with no paychecks. She contacted her mother and asked if we could come to stay with my grandparents, in Milwaukee. She agreed we could stay in their rear cottage; the tenants had moved. My father had to stay in the hospital six months as he had a broken hip, broken ribs, broken pelvis, broken wrist and some inner injuries.

Chapter 4

MOVE TO MILWAUKEE

We moved back to Milwaukee, how we got there, I really do not know. We did not have money for food. The little corner store, down the alley would give us credit for a week and I am sure my grandmother helped. Every Saturday the little baldheaded, Jewish grocer, with his long white apron on, would walk down the alley to the neighbors and try to collect some money. He had his little blue spiral notebook which told what each customer owed.

Christmas that year grandpa got us a tree. Daddy was still in the Shawano hospital. Mom did her best to make Christmas for Carl and me. We took the key to open the coffee cans and unwound them to make icicles for the tree and my grandfather's tobacco packages were shiny silver on the outside and we cut out stars. We took my grandpa's old ice pick to put holes for the hangers. These were our ornaments.

After several months, daddy came home and was on crutches for a while. He still could not work for some time. Dad finally got a job at a factory where his friend worked.

On weekends in the summer, the Jewish Sheeny man would come through every yard and call out, "Rags, rags." He had a cart that he pulled by hand and rang a little bell. He was a junk collector. When we misbehaved our parents told us that we would be sold to the Sheeny man.

The man selling fruit off his cart would come through the neighborhood. He had bananas that were overripe for cheap. We got a huge bunch.

Peddlers came through on the weekend because the wage earners were home, and the peddlers could collect more money.

Evenings, you heard the bell ring. Tinkle, tinkle, here comes the ice cream cart. If we got anything, it would be popsicles because there were two, one for each kid.

Saturday night was bath night. Mom would put my hair in rag curls for church Sunday morning.

Occasional weekdays, I would run to my grandmother's house in the front and my grandfather and I would have breakfast. He would have puffed wheat, but I liked puffed rice. My grandmother would put some milk in my hot water, so that I could drink with them, while they were having coffee. They mostly spoke German and I tried to act like I knew German.

One afternoon, Knock, knock there was a salesman at my grandmother's front door. My grandmother answered and he said that he was from a music studio and they were looking for new students. My mother and I happened to be at my grandmothers at the time. He asked if he could come in and see what instrument I might do well playing. He sat on my grandmother's over- stuffed sofa and turned my hands right side up and upside down and said that I would do well playing violin.

His boss taught violin, viola and cello. I was eight at the time. The deal was to take forty lessons and you would receive a new violin. My grandmother paid to let me take violin lessons. My mother and I went once a week, on the bus and I got the violin and case. I was the first grandchild and was doted over. My grandfather went to the basement, found some odd pieces of wood and made a music stand for me. He painted it green, probably the only paint in the basement. He sat in his old wood chair in the kitchen, by the window and I played violin for him. He would sing along, Old Black Joe and Comin' through the Rye. An old white-haired man of few words, but he would sing with me playing. He would later fall asleep in the chair and his lower false teeth would hang out. The beauty of Grandpa Otto.

He and I were sitting on the porch one day, on the bench. I was about eight or nine. He told me that my real father jumped off a bridge. I never had an idea why he told that to me.

I always needed busy work, my mother or grandmother would find mending, hemming and such. My mother liked me to wash clothes and clean house, maybe something she did not care to do.

My grandmother would suggest that I could go and trim the hedges or cut the grass. Saturdays, I would clean my grandma's house and dust the plate rail. I feel like I was born old, never wanting to do things kids do.

Being a first grandchild and a firstborn, I was constantly around adults only. I listened and learned a lot. I never did figure out why adults thought as they did.

A couple of years later, I was selected to be in All City Junior orchestra, we did not have the money for my mother and I to go on the bus every Saturday morning to practice so it was a no go.

Chapter 5

DINNER WITH RUTH AND JOE

*D*addy was a free spirit. He worked in the factory as a machinist. Any relative who came to town without a place to stay, could stay at our house for a while.

My dad had been married before. He had a son that was just seven months older than me and lived with his mother. His name was Paul. We were about twelve when he sent me a letter and wrote that we could get married. I never quite knew what he meant because we were not close. I let it go.

Every summer we would go to see Paul, on our vacation. Paul's mother Ruth, who was my father's first wife, and her husband, Joe would make dinner for our family. My mother and Ruth would sit and talk, and Ruth's second husband and my father would talk.

Dad paid $20 every month for support for Paul. He suspected but did not know that he was not the father. We kids would go out and play with Paul and enjoy the day.

Chapter 6

TRUTH UNCOVERED

I had many questions over the years and pieced them together. I was about thirteen when I decided to go to my mother and see what she had to say. I asked all my questions.

"I was afraid to tell you." She was fearing to tell me that Henry, the father I lived with since I could remember was not my biological father. They got married when I was two.

Her worries were for naught.

"That moment wasn't part of my life, it's part of your life. Henry was my dad since always."

"Would you like to see a picture of him?"

"I don't need to see it."

A tear rolled down her face, we were just silent for a bit and hugged.

"Mama it's alright, I love you."

Chapter 7

THE GOAT FARM

addy was an adventurous, dreamer of a man. He decided it was time to move again. We were constantly moving.

That summer, he met an old Jewish man that mentioned that he had a place out in Thiensville, and it was for rent. Why, oh why my father thought that was a good idea, I will never know.

Old man Altman would go from Second and Center Street in the city, to Thiensville each weekend. He was a short, bent over old man with a curly white head of hair. He always carried a huge grocery bag with handles. His wife would not leave the city. He took the Greyhound bus out to his weekend place.

It was a goat farm. Who fed the goats when he was not there, I will never know. The old shack we lived in only had an outhouse. Grandpa Altman as we called him, stayed upstairs. He ate off broken plates and drank goat milk. My brother would go up and drink goats' milk with him. Carl locked himself in the outhouse and did not know what to do. The old gentleman came and got him out.

I do remember it was a short stay because we never went to school there, and we only lived there one summer. What a summer it was. The old man had wire cages to catch all the rats that were in the barn. He drowned them in a huge pail of water near the barn. He taught my brother and I to take them by the tails and throw them against the barn. What kids think is fun.

Chapter 8

LIFE IN THE TAVERN

My father gets a new idea and this time the tavern he hung at every day, had the apartment attached to the tavern for rent. We moved again, only two blocks from my grandma's. There were two gray painted windows in the living room, connecting to the tavern.

Lucille, a good-looking lady with long burgundy curls, big breasts, and a great figure lived upstairs and was single. She would go into the bar every Saturday night. The men would buy her drinks and give her quarters to play the jukebox. All night she would play Cold Cold Heart. You could hear it through the two gray windows.

It was the only time my father was on time for dinner, because you could go out our screen door, take five steps and be at the back screen door of the tavern, all part of the same building. My mother would send my brother to go to get dad for dinner. We only lived there a year or two.

Chapter 9

SWINGING DOOR

*A*nother move. This time my grandmother getting older, my mother wanted to live near her mother. We moved in the upper flat my grandmother owned.

Mom made dinner every night and you knew which night was chicken, which night was meatloaf and which night was hard hamburgers. Everything had to be well done. We would cut the porkchops in half if necessary when company came at mealtime. Sunday's, daddy would make a beef roast, lots of onions and garlic. He was a great cook as he used to be the cook in a lumber camp.

Two of my cousins came to Milwaukee for work and moved in with us. Six people and one bathroom had its own issues. I continued to do the laundry. Several loads of laundry every week. All their laundry went into the laundry basket too. I wanted to help my mother and make it easier for her.

I barely remember ever acting as a child. Mom and I were always at odds because our way of thinking was opposite. I loved her to the ends of the earth, but she was easy to make cry. She had such a soft gentle spirit, and my spirit was always on fire. I would offer to take Carl to the park so I could see the boys.

"Yes, take your brother to the park."

You can imagine the life I was leading; never knowing from one day to the next where we would be living. What condition would my father be when he came home from the tavern every night. Mom always looking sad or with a tear in her eye. Still every night she would put her hair up in bobby pins and wrap a scarf around her hair. In the morning she would have a fresh wash dress on, and a little lipstick, that she blotted, and the percolator was ready. All before she woke my father.

It took a toll on me through the years making me wonder why adults made the decisions they made. I always wondered how I could make it better. He hollered and she cried every day. My bedroom was off the kitchen. No wonder I wet the bed until I was fourteen.

On Sundays, as we got older, my brother and I would pick a model of car, Ford or Chevy. The one with the most car count would be the winner. No prize but helped time pass. We stayed in the same school district throughout our moves.

I always thought we were middle-class because everyone I knew had less than we had. More than likely it was because we had my grandmother's help. We may not have had much money, but on a good Sunday, we would get the record player out. Our family would dance.

Chapter 10

MOM AND DAD'S MEETING

I asked my mother how my dad and she met.

"We met at the Eagle's Ballroom where there was dancing every weekend and a huge mirror ball hanging in the dance hall. That was our attraction."

Oh, maybe he drank a lot, did not have that good a job, but my mother knew he loved me. We came as a package. That was the driving force in her life, she told me.

"We decided to get married. Your father's divorce was not final, so we ran off to Waukegan, Illinois to get married."

Every Sunday, as the years went along, my dad saw to it we got to church and then he would leave for the tavern. When he came home, he would lay down for a nap. Mom always assigned either my brother or me to go and wake him up and see if we were going out to the lake, to his brother's cottage or if he were too crabby to bother, my brother, my mother and I would play Old Maid or Rummy.

Chapter 11

First Glimpse of Racial Issues

The houses were getting old and the value of homes went down, our neighborhood was changing. It had been mostly Germans and Jews.

A black family moved in. The parents were both professionals, had one daughter and probably had more money than all of us. The old people thought the neighborhood was going downhill now. Racial bias, my first glimpse. The community continued to change over the years.

In our last neighborhood, which I forgot about, one more of our many moves, our next-door neighbors were black. He and his wife were graduates of Marquette University. They were Catholics and had nine children. I babysat for them. The two twin boys, Kevin and Kurt would win every set of checkers. They were five years old.

When I was in grade school, on Fifth and Center it had about half white students and half black students.

Our family did not think about color. We were all poor and all lived in the same neighborhoods. Many households only had one parent. At the time, there were no guns, a few knives that's about it.

The twin's father, from our last neighborhood, would come to get me to babysit. One night he and his wife were going to a major event at his company. The old ladies across the street had to put their eyes back in their heads because they thought we were going on a date. More racial animosity.

My family, because of my father's open-mindedness, in every respect, did not know color or class. He left home at fourteen. He worked in the lumber camps in the state of Washington. Working with older men, he had to grow up quickly.

Saturday nights, the Cadillacs would pull up at the curb, beautiful young white women generally with blonde, long hair, and fur collared coats. They would get out of the car and a handsome black man would open their door. They would go in the duplex across the street.

One Sunday morning, I found capsules along the curb and brought them to my mother. She grabbed them and threw them away. My brother played across the street with the boy from the duplex.

"Mom, mom Griffin has a big wheel in his living room." Mom understood it was a roulette wheel.

I hung the laundry in the attic. On Monday, I was up there, hanging the clothes and looked out the two narrow, tall windows up front. My eyes glared. In the same house across the street upstairs, a lady had moved in a couple of mattresses and two little boys. There was a beautiful specimen of a black man in her bay window, no clothes, standing with a great physique and well endowed. I was a young teenager. I ran down to the second floor to tell my mother.

She insisted that she would hang the rest of the clothes. Next-door, in the rear cottage a young white couple lived. They maybe were 20 years old, two little boys and two motorcycles.

It seemed after school there were crowds of young people constantly going there. I much later found out they were shooting up.

Across the alley, there was another house, with white and black girls and guys and later I found out it was a drug ring. I never felt fearful of living in that neighborhood. The groups stuck to their own, never bothered the rest of us.

Time for seventh and eighth graders from my school to be the first, to be incorporated with the North high school. I went there seventh, eighth, ninth, and 10th grades.

I was having some difficulty being only one of six white students in the school, and only a few white girls. I was an attraction, and something different to some of the black boys. None of the black boys that were bothering me were my dear friends from the grade school.

I was being grabbed in the hallways and on the play-ground, I began to feel unsafe. I had lasted four years and finally told my mom and she went to the principal and he agreed that I could go to the Eastside high school for my last two years.

The only issue that I did not know, neither did my mother know, that on the transfer slip, the principal stated that I wished to be with a different racial group. Race was not our issue, it was safety.

Chapter 12

IVIED WALLS AND BARRED WINDOWS

At the new school when the Dean of Girls read the transfer slip, she called me into the office. "We have 10 black students in this school and if you had not bothered those boys, they would not have bothered you." I was speechless.

I sat there shaking and sick to my stomach because I loved my black friends. I had no racial issues, I only had safety issues. She sat me right in the front desk in her homeroom. I did not want to go to school.

I have always been against bussing because of my personal experience. When I arrived at the East side school, the students mainly had professional parents. It was a whole different ballgame because in English this school concentrated on literature, whereas the school I came from had to, in English class concentrate on the grammar.

Dad had no schooling, never attended school. He could not read nor write. In the case of many of the kids in my neighborhood, the parents were not that well-educated and had to work. Many came from one parent families and so lived a different life. My experience was that in algebra, the school was 70 pages ahead and in Latin, the same.

I am used to getting excellent grades because my father who had no education insisted, we do well. You do not argue with your father out of fear and you get the grades.

The Latin teacher said that I could come to her after school and she would tutor me. My algebra teacher then said that I could come in the morning early and she would tutor me. My mother said that I wanted to quit school when I first got there. I always implied, "ivied walls and barred windows."

Without the help of these two women, I could not have stayed. I finally was able to bring up my grades. My feeling is, this was not a racial situation but a socio-economic situation. The students at the new school, had cars and most had enough money to buy lunch every day or go somewhere on the weekends. The students, like myself that came from the other side of the river, in other words transferees, barely had money to buy a school pass as we had to travel on the city bus, to get to the new school. I did get to go to a few proms, the bit of pleasure I did have during these years. Weekends I usually had a date. We dated on the bus. Boys I dated didn't have cars.

We the students from the north side were not accepted by the students who lived on the east side. We seemed to them to be invaders and low life. I hadn't been to a restaurant until I was asked on a date. It was no real problem as my mother and my grandmother had always taught me manners. We did not have money, but we did have class.

Mom gave me a quarter a day in the summer for doing chores to go to the pool at Gordon Park. I walked two miles to get there and two miles back home. A relief to get away from my home life and have the boys attracted to me.

Chapter 13

TRAGEDY STRIKES

*G*raduation came and now to find a job. First to go on a family vacation to see my father's relatives on their farms. My mom, dad, brother and I, took the two-hour drive to Shawano.

You always had to get mentally prepared, as my father did not read nor write; we had to read every sign along the way. When we forgot to read a Burma-Shave sign, all chaos broke loose. Daddy began to blast out, because to him it might have read Road Out.

We would stop halfway in order to use the restroom at a gas station. In the car, my mother had packed sliced bolonga and a package of frosted cinnamon buns. I will never know why she picked that combination.

When we got there, it was thrashing time. The farmers were bringing in the grain. Our aunt Elaine made the highest Lemon Meringue pies, and they were mouthwatering. Her loaves of bread seemed two feet tall. They were huge and airy.

We had a wonderful vacation, visiting all the relatives. It was a whole week of peace. It probably was my last trip before I needed to find a job. My brother wanted to stay another week with his cousins. My folks agreed. We left and I was in total charge of sign reading for my dad on the way home. Now back to real life.

About midweek, the phone rang. I picked it up.

"This is the Shawano County Sheriff's Department. Is Mr. Henry Williamson there?"

I gave my father the phone and he almost passed out. He started screaming,

"No, no, no. It just can't be, it just can't be."

My brother Carl had drowned. All of us went hysterical.

We had to go back to Shawano. My good friend, Bill offered to drive us there, because my family couldn't function. When we got to my aunts, she told us the cousins had been out swimming in the Wolf River. They were fooling around when my brother called out. The cousins thought he was kidding and went home. My cousin asked his mother, "Where is Carl?" "He never came home."

They called the police, and several other relatives went out to the river. The authorities dragged the river and finally found him. My brother had been a good swimmer. My cousins needed counseling after that.

I had to take charge because no one in my family was able. I made all the arrangements. Carl and I were not just siblings; we were best friends. We later found out that my brother got a cramp in his leg, and that is how he drowned.

Life in our house was never the same. My father always lived with the unnecessary blame for leaving my brother up there. My mother was forever changed also. The loss of a child, no one should be asked to bear.

I decided to stay tough, but my friend Bill reminded me I would have to come down. Finally, the flood waters flowed, and I cried most of the day.

Being my father's child, I picked up the pieces and carried on.

Chapter 14

STRESS OVERWHELMS

I was job hunting every day. I lived at home, and each morning I got up I had the chills and was sick to my stomach. My bedroom was off the kitchen and my parents argued every morning.

My mother thought I should go to the doctor and see what was wrong with me. At eighteen, the old German doctor gave me an internal exam and informed his nurse, "It is so tight nothing would fit up there."

When I told my parents, they laughed. I was totally embarrassed. The doctor sent me to the hospital to get checked. Nine days later and every test, I had seen every young intern in my room. The doctor's report,

"We find nothing is wrong."

They sent in the psychiatrist and he told me,

"It's between God and you, and you better do your share."

Horrible what stress can do to a person. I could not figure life out. I had had it and went on a date with my boyfriend the night I got out of the hospital.

I landed a job at a factory. I moved out into an apartment with Della that I worked with at the factory. I stayed there for about a year. I moved back home and decided to change jobs. I got hired at Northwestern Mutual Life Insurance company. I worked in death claims and killed people. Literally I stamped deceased on their card.

Chapter 15

ENTER BRAD

Saturday my mom suggested we go over to see her best high school friend, Mildred. They would be lifelong friends. Mildred's father owned a plumbing company on Center Street. Mildred and her husband rented an apartment in the building. Her son was home. I got to meet him. His name was Brad. His eyes and mind quite caught my eye immediately. He was tall, wavy dark hair and a sparkle in his big, brown eyes. It came out that we had both gone to the same school, but he graduated a year before me. Funny I had never noticed him.

"Are you going to the homecoming game next Saturday?"

"I don't know yet."

"Would you like to go with me?"

"Okay."

Once I got out of school, I never cared to go to a game, but I did want to go on a date with Brad. I never knew it would be the beginning of a year-long relationship. He was crazy about me from the get-go, but I never seemed to have the same feeling for him. We were always crazy necking and petting in the car, but I would never let him go all the way. I knew my mother had me before she was married, and I knew it would crush her if the same thing happened to me.

"My sister is getting married on June 22nd. Keep the date open."

Brad's sister, Mary was getting married in Chicago. Brad and his cousins Josh and Jake would stand up for the wedding. The day came and the girls all wore Hunter's green, street length Peau de Soie satin gowns. The bouquets had mini yellow and white carnations, with Ivy and dark green trailing ribbons. It was a gorgeous reception at the Ambassador Hotel.

In the evening we all went to the reception. As the evening went on, Brad was talking to some people across the room, and Jake asked me to dance. As we danced, our eyes caught and there was instant chemistry. We danced about three dances, and Brad came over and tapped me on the shoulder and insisted,

"Let's dance."

I guess he didn't like it that Jake and I were connecting. On the way home, there was silence. I could tell Brad was upset with me. He dropped me off rather abruptly that night. I knew my feelings could never seem to heat up.Brad was in love with me. He loved me from the day he met me, I knew he was a special guy. I did not have the same feelings for him. He did not call for a few days and then we reconnected.

He came over one morning, on a Saturday and told me that he decided to sign up for the Air Force. He came from a military family and he always wanted to go in service. In their family, it was expected that every man should serve. I felt terrible.

"How long will you be gone?"

"It will be a two-year assignment."

We fought about that for many days and finally I knew I would never win. The military went back three generations in his family. One almost had to serve.

We had one last night to be together. The guys had a party for him, and we drank quite a bit.

He begged me and begged me, in the car,

"Just give it to me once before I go. It's our last night. Just once can't hurt anything."

"I don't think I can." His wet kisses were so persuasive, and I had had too much to drink. He was so gentle and sweet that I stopped resisting. I later thought sex must be overrated, I was uncomfortable.

Brad came over in the morning and we were both grabbing for the tissue box, and he left on that Tuesday afternoon.

Next morning, I was lonesome, even though I knew we would never get married. I knew how much he loved me; I did not feel the same.

Brad went to Sumter South Carolina to Shaw Air Force Base. I wrote him a letter but knew he could not get mail until after basic so I would have to wait to send it out.

Chapter 16

OH, OH TROUBLE APPEARS

The next Saturday afternoon my mom asked me to carry some things that she had for Mildred over to her house. Mildred said that she already missed Brad terribly. Brad was her only son, more than I missed him.

That day Jake had come up from Chicago to see some friends and he stopped at his aunt Mildred's while I was there. Wow, the chemistry was still there.

"It's such a nice day, would you like to go for a drive Marie, in my convertible?"

"Okay."

We drove down Lake Drive and parked at the lake, at Necker's Point. The seagulls were all over. The waves were towering that day over and onto the sand. We got out, took our shoes off, and ran through the sand. We laughed and giggled so hard and so long our stomach's ached. He grabbed me and touched my breast over my blouse.

"My mother will wonder where I am. We better get going." He leaned over and kissed my cheek. "You are right, I don't know what I might do." I knew my feelings too. My heart was pounding, my stomach had butterflies. Wow, already I was crazy about him.

He dropped me off at my moms, but before I got out of the car, he reminded me that the Lakefront in Milwaukee was having a boat event next weekend.

"I know you're seeing Brad, but we can go as friends." I thought about it, for only a moment, knowing I should not but, I had to go.

"Okay, if we can go as only friends, I'm on."

"Okay, pick you up on Saturday morning at ten, at your moms. I will be staying at my aunts for the weekend and maybe we can go again on Sunday. It only comes once a year."

I could not sleep that night. I knew better than to go, but he just made my heart sing.

Only as friends was the deal, no problem.

I thought the week would never be over till Saturday.

As promised Saturday at ten, Jake arrived. Great jeans, black T-shirt, wavy black hair, great muscles. I thought my heart stopped. He looked, like I could eat him up. We parked and I could not believe it, we stayed all day. My feet were getting tired. We decided to have some corn on the cob and the butter was dripping all over. He patted my face to dry off the butter. He was slowly putting the tip of the cob of corn into his mouth and pulling it back out. I picked up that was a sexual thing. I still had to remember, just friends.

We listened to Caribbean music. We were dancing in the grass. We even got out a blanket and stayed for the fireworks. The time got away and I thought it was a week rather than a day; we crammed in so much fun and I got in late.

"For friends you sure spend a lot of time together."

"Oh mom!"

I woke up the next morning and thought what did I do? For friends we sure had a good time. He was thoughtful and caring and handsome.

Sunday morning, he called "What a fabulous time I had. Let's go back to the lakefront. My brother Josh has a sailboat rented for the day. Please oh please. I know "just friends." The water was a blue green. The breeze was gentle. We packed ham sandwiches and some beer. The day was romantic, oh, oh. It was late.

Before Jake kissed me goodnight, he mentioned, "Next weekend in Chicago the art museum is exhibiting Cezanne."

"I have to think about it" only because I was caring too much and was still in a relationship with Brad.

It only took one day, I called him. "I will go but remember just as friends."

"You could stay for the weekend and I would sleep on the sofa, and you could have my bed because it will be a big weekend in Chicago.

Whoa, so much too soon. I had to think about it. My mother was concerned. She could see by the look in my eyes that I was intrigued, seriously intrigued with Jake.

The weekend could not come soon enough. I took the Amtrak to Chicago, and Jake met me there. We spent part of the day shopping at Bloomingdale's and Nordstrom's and went to eat lunch at a small café on Michigan Avenue. In the afternoon we strolled down Michigan Avenue looking at all the store windows and enjoying being together.

Evening came and time to go to Jake's place, and I now realized what I committed to. I was shocked when he put the key in the door and flung it open. Everything was in order and the apartment must've had a decorator. It was beautiful. He had a leather sofa that had a sleeper in it. His place overlooked the city, and you could see all the city lights.

"Where do you work and what do you do?"

"I am a financial advisor at Wm. Blair and Co."

We sat on the sofa and talked the night away. The more we talked, the closer we sat, the more we laughed. The night was waning and after the last drink it was time to go to bed. He showed me his room, and the master bath that I could use for myself.

I brushed my teeth and got in my robe and he came in to say good night. He kissed me on the forehead, looked at me in my long pink robe. Jake grabbed me and kissed the living daylights out of me.

"I am so sorry, I got carried away." He left and went out to the sleeper sofa, pulled it out and fell fast asleep.

Next morning, when I woke up, he was already out in the kitchen getting breakfast ready for me.

"You are just so cute in the morning."

I smiled "Friends remember, just friends."

He laughed "Oh yeah I forgot", with this guilty smile on his face.

We both got dressed and started our Sunday. There was a lot going on in Chicago today. First stop we went to see the Cezanne exhibit. There were many still life's and portraits. In the early afternoon we decided to go to the planetarium. He suggested we go back to his place with the tamale's we had picked up from a street vendor. We ate and then it was time for me to catch the Amtrak back to Milwaukee. Jake drove me there. We got there early and reminisced about what a great time we both enjoyed. Jake and I knew we were in trouble. The chemistry was sizzling, and I knew Brad was not the one.

The next day my mother queried,

"Don't you think you're going a little deep with this new friendship, you remember you are in a relationship."

"Mom I always kind of felt that Brad was not the one. He was in love with me, but I never was in love with him."

"Listen to your heart. There were times when I did not, and still carry regrets."

Jake called midweek.

"I had a great time. I know friends, just friends but what a special friend. Our friendship is better than some of my relationships in the past."

"Likewise. Got to go, am going to the gym now."

"Can I call you again?"

"Gotta go now, bye."

Friday Jake called again. "I know it's a lot, but I need someone to go to a business event in Chicago for my company. Everyone brings a partner; would you go with me?"

"When is the event?"

"Tomorrow evening, I was afraid to call you."

"Let me call you back when I get back from the gym, and if you agree that it's just friends. Is it a dress-up occasion?"

"Yes, formal is that what you mean, yes, it is."

"I do have a dress that I thought would fit the occasion. I will come on the Amtrak, if again you will pick me up."

"It's a deal."

Saturday morning, I caught the Amtrak. When I arrived, Jake waved to me and I ran to him. He gave me a big bear hug when he picked me up.

"Thank you so much, I would've had to go alone, and I would have been the only one alone."

We went to his apartment, had a glass of wine and had to get ready to go to the gala. I had my long blonde hair pulled back in a low large black satin bow midway to my shoulders. My dress was black velvet, spaghetti strap, long with a side slit up the leg. I wore smoky gray hose, and black pumps.

I came out of the bedroom; his eyes became saucers.

"Oh, you are a Renaissance woman, extraordinaire. You have the most magnificent blue eyes, like the waters of the Caribbean. I never had this experience with a friend, I know just friends."

Time to go, he had a car pick us up so we could be dropped off and picked up. We arrived at the Drake and I was introduced to many of Jake's associates; they appeared to be all staring at me.

We later got talking with them, they were telling me they had not seen Jake with a woman in a long time. Jake and I strolled over to the chocolate fountain and talked. We each dipped a strawberry in the chocolate fountain and fed each other.

There was a band, and we danced all night after dinner. I had never been in this kind of company before, but it fit me like hand in glove. Did I die and go to heaven, and was I going to wake up in the morning and it was all a dream?

We got back to the house, I wanted to get into something more comfortable and take my dress off. I could not get the zipper down, it appeared stuck.

"Jake can you unzip me?" I had a black bra with ivory lace at the bottom edge, and he undid that also.

"Jake, we can't, remember, friends." He grabbed me, kissed me and threw me on the bed. We started laughing, hugging, kissing and just stopped; and fell fast asleep in each other's arms.

Next morning, I woke up and asked, "What got into us last night? You know we've got to stop this."

"I think you need to write to Brad and let him know. It's the right thing to do."

I took the Amtrak back to Milwaukee late on Sunday and knew I had to write the letter.

Sunday night, I couldn't sleep and began the letter to Brad, I had to get the address from Mildred. I kept writing and crossing out. I am seeing someone else; I am sure he knew it was Jake. I worded it very carefully as not to hurt him, but I knew it would. I cannot really imagine how he felt because I know he was in love with me. I never heard from him again. His mother Mildred heard from him occasionally. I do not think she knew what to say to me. She always liked me, and she loved her son. We never talked about Brad again. Maybe my mother and she spoke about us, but never to me.

Jake and I decided one night to run off and get married. We backed out. When we came back and told our mothers that we were going to get married real soon, both mothers thought we lost our minds.

We decided to appease them and have a real wedding. I wanted to be with Jake all the time, and as he lived in Chicago, I wanted to live there. I had seen my future wedding dress about a year before when my girlfriend got married. She had the perfect dress, I called her and asked if she would sell it to me. She did.

I was ready to get on with the wedding. Dad asked me, "Who's walking you down the aisle?" I begged, "Aren't you?" He teary-eyed smiled.

It was a small wedding with family members. Jake and I were madly in love and nothing else mattered. We were tied at the hip. We went every place together. We could never get enough of each other. Monday, I did not go to work because I was sick to my stomach. Maybe we ate too much. The next day I felt better. I had to give my notice at work so I could move with Jake. He lived in Chicago and we decided to move into his apartment.

Mom said, "If you are happy, I am happy Marie. An eagle needs a right wing and a left-wing to fly. The two of you will need to work together."

Chapter 17

PINK ARRIVAL

*N*ow reality set in. It was quite an adjustment for Jake having a roommate. I really was not that good a cook, many times Jake would bring carryout home. I started a job at Bloomingdale's. One evening when Jake came home, I needed to figure out how to tell him my thoughts.

"Jake, I have something to tell you. I don't know, but I think I could be pregnant."

"Marie, are you sure?"

"I don't know but I missed my period a couple of times. I guess I was not paying attention lately. I never have been regular, but I have been feeling queasy."

"For God sakes darlin', go to the doctor. You just cannot be pregnant, you just cannot."

Jake knew when he was a kid, he had had rheumatic fever and the doctors said he probably would never have children. Jake was ecstatic that they were

53

wrong. The following week I went to the doctor and sure enough, I really was pregnant. We both had to inhale the whole idea, but no doubt we loved each other and would deal with it.

We just couldn't stop hugging and kissing to know we would be three. Jake had a great job; money was no issue.

I worked for several months. Jake came home and had news.

"I have a great new job offer. It's in Groton, Connecticut."

"Really? I guess you need to check it out."

When I told my mother, she could not believe we possibly would be moving away before the baby was born.

Jake and I flew out to Groton. He took the job, and we found a house. Both of us could not believe that we rarely disagreed. Jake mentioned that we had an unusual fairytale relationship and marriage. Moving day came. Mom cried and we all hugged.

When we got to our new home, we had to get furniture and got a decorator to help. We did some remodeling for our tastes. Jake put me in charge of the inside and said he would take care of outside. We enjoyed the small town feel of Groton. We enjoyed the Seafood restaurants and friendly natives. Jake brought lobster rolls home often for dinner, my favorite.

I woke up early one morning and had severe pains. I looked at the clock and they were coming five minutes apart. It was a couple of months before the baby was due, but five minutes apart. I woke Jake. "I need to go to the hospital."

"Are you sure, Marie?"

"For sure Jake."

Three hours later, we had a baby girl.

The doctor said, "She is amazing for a preemie, but everything looks good." We already had picked out the name Ann Marie, as we knew it would be a girl. She weighed 6 lbs. 7 oz. and had a solid head of curly black hair.

My mother flew out for a week when our daughter Ann arrived. It was a touchy week because my mother and I were a bit abrasive to each other from time to time. She was concerned about the baby because she had come so early. I told her that the doctor said she is fine and not to worry. I was going to be a stay-at-home mom. She knew Jake and I could handle it alone and flew home. Jake was such a good dad and was the one who got up during the night. He was as proud as he could be. He only had a brother and so did I. We were ecstatic to have a girl in the family.

Chapter 18

CATHERINE'S LIFE CHANGES

After a while, I wondered why I had not heard from my mother for quite some time. The phone rang. It was mom. She could barely speak. Her voice was trembling.

"Is Jake with you?"

"Yes.

"You need to sit down. Your dad went for his physical today, the doctor said everything was normal. He got to the parking lot of the doctor's office and collapsed. The woman getting into the next car came over and called 911. The ambulance came, but it was too late. They could not revive him. They said it was a heart attack.

"It can't be dad isn't that old. Mom, are you alright?"

It took me aback. I knew things had not been going well with my folks for quite some time, but not this. I was in shock. Jake needed to hold me. I needed to call mom back later when I could speak. I called mom the next day. She and I made all the decisions. We flew back for the funeral with the baby. My mom needed medication to get her through.

Mildred was there for my mom and when she saw the baby, she said how beautiful she was and that her daughter, Mary had been bald, but Brad had curly black hair when he was born. Good thing Mildred was there, as my mom just couldn't think straight.

We talked often after that because I was concerned for my mom being alone.

About six months after my dad passed my mom called us.

"I will be moving into my own apartment next month. I have decided to move from the memories. I love downtown, that's where I'm going to live. The apartment building is called the Downtowner. It overlooks the lake which I love."

Mom started her new life in downtown Milwaukee. She shared with me that she had told her mother that there were three things she wanted to do in her life from the time she was thirteen. Mom said that since she was a small child, she had a will of her own. She had told her mom those three things were, she wanted to be a social worker, to have a dress shop, and marry a minister. She told me that both her parents thought she had a screw loose at that age trying to plan her whole life. She was intent that someday that was all going to happen.

Mom said there was no way she was going to live like her parents did with no money and no dreams, all those things would have to happen. I guess the idea of marrying a minister, came from the fact that our minister, every Sunday had a message that would last for a week, until the next Sunday. He was such a beautiful person inside and out. His Thanksgiving's sermon was, to be thankful for dirty dishes.

I was so busy with taking care of things for Ann, getting her to gymnastics, ballet and music lessons that I had hardly had time for myself. I had always been taking many pictures throughout Ann's life and sending them to mom as Ann was the only grandchild. Jake seemed to always be working. He was there when I needed him.

Ann approached me.

"Isn't it funny you and dad have such light-colored hair, and mine is nearly black. You guys have blue eyes and I have brown."

"Yeah, but it does happen in several families." We let it go at that.

I called mom to see how her new life was working. She was telling me that she started to think about her life on the overall and started recalling and replanning her life. I could tell mom had healed. Going forward, mom seemed to keep her life more to herself and was spending her time with Millie. Mom seemed to want to tell her stories to her. Jake and I were quite busy or traveling. She was working on writing her autobiography.

She invited Mildred over to her new apartment.

"Cat, when Brad's dad decided to move on, you were with me through all of that, and now with Henry's passing, I'm here for you."

"Millie you and I are going to start having some fun after I adjust to my newfound life. I am worn out of the whole change."

I wanted to sleep a great deal. Henry's death, the move, and the thought of my different life were overwhelming.

In the meanwhile, I was outlining the ideas for a boutique someday. I had read in the Architectural Digest of the first boutique in Paris that Elsa Schiaparelli had opened in 1927. I started to write more poetry and even dabbled in my artwork. I enjoyed oil painting. The boutique was constantly on my mind.

Elsa's boutique was unique. A princess and several wealthy women became consultants at Elsa's because it quickly became the place to be and be seen.

Chapter 19

LIFE FULL OF SURPRISES

A month went by and all I wanted to do stay in my apartment. I took a walk on Jefferson Street and saw a sign for rent, on this charming old building. It was the perfect place for a dress shop. I walked a block to the Pfister Hotel piano bar. The music was soothing and because it was early in the afternoon, I had a Bloody Mary.

I walked the block back to the old building. I called the number on the side, a man answered. He agreed to show the place.

It was perfect, years ago it had been a home. I had to make the decision. I called Millie to see what she thought.

"You always wanted to do this why not now?"

The next day I stopped for lunch at Elsa's on the Park. I met with Louise my friend. I enjoyed a pork chop sandwich with teriyaki sauce, grilled onions, pecans and bleu cheese dressing. My favorite there. She encouraged me to open the boutique.

Later in the afternoon I stopped at my mailbox in the lobby, and there was a business envelope. Return address was from a law firm in New York. I took the elevator to my apartment and tore open the envelope. It read RE: estate of James R. Lewis/Catherine M Williamson. Please call my office immediately to discuss this matter.

"Mr. Köstenberger, please. This is Catherine Williamson. You called about Mr. Lewis. I do not know Mr. Lewis."

"He evidently knows you. You need to come to my office in New York."

"I will call you back." I needed more information before I would fly to New York.

I decided to call my aunt, my mother's sister, Emma, who lived in New York, to see if she knew anything about this law firm or Mr. Lewis. My parents had been gone a long time. Emma was close to my mom and was my go-to person since then. I told her about the letter.

She went silent.

"Are you still there?"

"Oh yeah, I don't know where to start. Your mother was incredibly young, she felt you didn't need to know this. Now, I feel the need to explain.

James R. Lewis was head of a large fashion house in New York, Cara Carolina. Your mother was the lead seamstress. Only one night, they went to bed and she got pregnant. James business was going gangbusters. He was crazy about Clara, but James was not ready to be bothered at the time with anything that was going to interfere with his prosperous venture. He gave her a great deal of cash and sent her on her way.

She stayed at his company for a short while, but he did not want people to know about the baby coming. Your mom left and started working at a small newspaper. One night she was out with some friends and they suggested she should go back to be with her family. She decided to go back to Milwaukee.

It was all a lot to consider. I loved my other father Otto, the one I lived with all my life. He was all I ever knew no matter what, I always loved him. I went limp. I needed to give this some thought. It was too much for me. He was the only father I ever knew.

Hearing the whole story, I called the lawyer and made an appointment.

I flew to New York, stayed in the hotel overnight. The next morning, I met with Attorney Aaron Köstenberger. He informed me that Mr. James R Lewis, my biological father, had left me all his assets. In checking, I found out he had no other living relatives. I am glad I was sitting because I was overtaken. Mr. Köstenberger informed me that the amount of assets that would be mine, would need me to get an accountant to make sure how to handle all of James estate.

I flew back to Milwaukee, I called Millie and told her the captivating story. She could not believe it, I could not either. Millie was telling me her woes. She rarely hears from Brad. She said she had sent him a couple of pictures of Jake and Marie's baby so he could stay in the loop. She had always liked Marie and thought Brad and Marie would get married. Millie told me that she sent Ann birthday cards. I felt the same about Brad. She was surprised at my news. I told her I made the decision and was getting the boutique ready to open and sort out my private life.

I was still in disbelief. I threw myself across the bed. Otto was the only father I ever knew. He was such a great dad; a girl could not have asked for anymore. He treated my mother well and the same with me. Otto always treated me as his own. I was his own in spirit. I had few moments when I did not love him. If I did my mother reminded me, he goes to work every day to put food on our table.

It was a lot to absorb and I was not sure I was quite ready to accept this truth and different life. Going forward money would never be an issue which would help to get the boutique set up. I was used to spending my money carefully and wisely. Henry had never made that much money, we had to be cautious.

My life was an uproar. I really did not know, without the accountant, what to do with all those assets and my new reality. The boutique was getting all set up. I was able to have a lady, Maureen work part time to get started.

Chapter 20

SILVER SLIPPER

I rented it a month before it opened. Inside on the glass door, in script, I had the words Silver Slipper, "a touch of France" with a spike high heel shoe below. All in glittery silver. I had the glass counter put in for the jewelry display and put a French phone on the counter. The room already had a fireplace. Above the archway to the next room the sign read, Le Salon. Across the archway between rooms and down the sides were wine-colored taffeta drapes puddled to the floor. I had an outdoor light post lit at the archway with a hanger and a dress hanging on it. The next room had a wall of mirror and in front of the mirror, two golden ropes hanging to have dresses spinning. The third room had sachets, candles and all the pretty little tchotchkes.

Silver Slipper was an instant success. Ladies would come on their lunch hour to see new merchandise. Word spread like wildfire. I needed to hire a full-time girl to keep up with the schedule. Maureen and I would go to market in Chicago, to hunt for clothes Milwaukee had not yet seen.

Outside I painted the railings gold along the staircase and placed speakers so that the music could be heard by passersby. I always played French music, a little Edith Piaf. The ivory brick building was built in 1900. At Christmas speakers would play the Porter music box Christmas cassettes to attract new clients. Pine greens were entwined along the railings.

I love people, many times we would get into deep discussions about their lives. I had a sign on me that said, "tell me." With continued success, three girls now worked for me and made the money. I attracted the customers.

I was a street counselor all my life. I think that is where my fulfillment of being a social worker fit in as well as being a clairvoyant. Without the girls that sold merchandise, I would have been dead in the water. My spirituality carried me. I always had enough because I cared more about others than myself. I was never without. I was glad it was Friday and I needed to relax.

Chapter 21

A New Man

I gave it a lot of thought being it was Friday night, as I was putting a key in the door, I had on my mind that I was going for a fish fry even if I had to go alone. I had to detox. The man across the hall, whom I had seen several times in the building, was coming out his door across the hall.

"Hello".

"Hello, I'm going out for dinner, I don't know where yet."

"I am too, would you like to join me?"

"I would like that."

He was all dressed up in a suit. I had seen him many mornings in the parking structure, going to work with his briefcase.

He decided we would go to Katerina's, an Italian restaurant he frequented often. They knew him by first name. He ordered a bottle of Pinot Grigio for dinner and asked if that would be all right.

I didn't know the names of wines.

"Oh yes, that would be fine."

"What would you like for dinner?" I just met the man, did not know what to say.

"Might I suggest scallops and scampi."

"Yes, scallops."

"Would you like a drink before dinner?"

"I'll have a Brandy Manhattan with olives."

He told me that he moved here from West Virginia, for a new job. He would not have been my usual date, because he weighed 300 pounds. He had snow white hair, and a fine white mustache. He was of eloquent speech and treated me as a fine woman. After dinner he asked if I would like to go to listen to some jazz music and dance. Well okay, I could not say no. I needed a night out and it seemed like he did too.

It was late when we finally arrived home. He left me at the door and went across to his door. The next day, I found a yellow sticky note on my door that said your friend Sally, the dry cleaner, told me to say hi to you. The following day I put a sticky note on his door and that said Sally told me your shirts are ready. Third day there was a note on my door saying I make a wonderful angel hair pasta and I would come over and make it for you, if you like.

The following day we met in the hallway and agreed he would make dinner at my place. I lit the candles, he worked the kitchen and served me dinner. He did make a huge mess. I was glad to clean up after he had made dinner. We seemed to share dinner quite often after that.

Sam and I started seeing each other frequently. I was busy with the boutique. Sam had been about to give up on his life, so overweight and had just had all his teeth pulled and got his false teeth.

He was curious that my husband had been a factory worker, and I was an interior designer. I said that he was a great dancer. I felt no need to say more.

I had to go to my accountant, who had been a friend for several years, as to how I would place my money. We had several meetings to work out all details. Going forward, my life would be drastically changed.

When Sam and I met, we were a breath of fresh air to each other. I was not used to a man thinking that I was a dynamite woman, an intelligent woman and thought I was stunning. Every weekend we dined Friday night, Saturday night and Sunday night at all fine restaurants. He would not set a foot in a McDonald's. No wonder he weighed so much. He loved to eat and loved to cook. We enjoyed each other's company. He was Vice President of a law firm.

After a few months, Sam had to go to a convention in Absecon, New Jersey, to a golf resort, Seaview. He asked me to join him on the trip. The girls were able to handle the boutique, I agreed to go.

I was not used to this way of life with high styling every night. It was a life I could only have dreamt of and I found it fit me perfect. I had to buy some outfits because every night of the trip was formal.

We had to drive to New Jersey because he had all the boxes of golf balls for the tournament. I did not know he had narcolepsy. He would fall asleep at the wheel.

"Sam are you, all right?"

It was my first road trip with him. I was scared, I told him I would drive all the way back.

When we got there everyone thought that I was such a wonderful person and were just waiting to meet me. I was astounded because I was being the same person I always was, and I was used to being criticized for being different, not that bright and very eccentric.

These people, who were attorneys with their own firms and their spouses thought I was intriguing. I went up to the hotel room and hysterically sobbed. I was by myself.

How could this have happened to me, that this large group of people, all treated me so different than I was used to being treated. I was not putting on airs, being my usual self. It was wonderful being with people that got me. Sam and I took many trips during our time together. Thanks to Mr. Lewis I could hire help to keep the boutique working.

We would go about three times a year to his conventions. I recall going to New Orleans, having breakfast at Brennan's, dinner at Galatoires and beignets at Café Du Monde.

Could not leave New Orleans without a trip down Bourbon Street and art around Jackson Square. I remember several other trips, staying at the Mills House in Charleston South Carolina. We flew to Laguna Beach, California.

We stayed at Doral in Miami Beach, Florida and walked along South Beach.

In Virginia, we went to see the Holocaust Museum. It was awful, the elevator was a gas chamber, seeing all those old suitcases and old shoes lying around. We visited Colonial Williamsburg.

My favorite trip was when we stayed at the Waldorf Astoria in New York. Every night we ate at fabulous restaurants. We dined at the Café des Artiste, Sign of the Dove, Russian Tea Room and Le Cirque. Every night we would meet at the Mosaic, the lobby of the hotel or Peacock Alley, the lounge.

This night there were eight of us. Sam and I were guests of Michael and his bride. Outside the hotel, awaited a limousine and took us to Club 21 for dinner. The limousine waited outdoors and after dinner took us to a Cuban club called SOB. We danced to Cuban music until 3 AM. The limousine still waited and finally took us back to the Waldorf.

During the day, the men would go to their meetings, and we girls would go shopping on Madison Avenue. I took a day to walk to the Frick Museum. I wore my fur coat as it was chilling.

After a few years, I knew Sam and I would never live together. His house was always a mess. He always dozed off in the chair with a lit cigarette. When he got his shirts back from the cleaners, he would just throw the wrappings and pins on the floor. He never opened his mail. It sat on the chair and then he wondered why they were turning his electricity off. Maybe because he had not paid his bill in three months. I realized I was ready to move on and I did. In all of that we never lived together.

Chapter 22

TURN IN DIRECTION

The boutique was popular in town. The TV station came and did a feature on the Silver Slipper. A couple of different times the newspaper ran articles on the shop. We featured a one-day trip to New York on Midwest Express. I had booked the entire plane. What a fun experience to gather around the Rockefeller Center Christmas tree.

A boutique client of mine Joan came in one evening and said she knew a French man whom she thought I might like to meet. I thought it over and decided I would. She told him about me, and he said he would like to meet me. She said we would all meet at a small bar called the Appaloosa on the outskirts of the city. It was a Friday night; I would never forget. The night was very foggy, and it was some distance to go for me.

I followed Joan's directions and I was on a residential street. I saw some blue lights back from the road, but the name was different. I pulled in the gravel drive and went into the rickety old place There were some gruff guys at the horseshoe bar, with flannel shirts, baseball hats, having a beer and laughing loud.

The waitress behind the bar had a rough voice, long blonde hair and an old red shirt. She seemed to have an attitude.

In my small voice, I begged, "I am so lost. I am looking for the Appaloosa."

"Honey sit down." I was shaking, not knowing where I was at and not sure of these characters at the bar and there was a guy in the corner with a guitar wearing a cowboy hat, singing someday we will all just be a picture in a frame. The bar had a new name.

At that moment Joan came and I didn't know what Ken looked like, not sure if he was already there. She and I ordered a drink; I was facing her.

"Ken just came in the door," she said.

He came around my right side.

"Oh wow!!!" I guess he thought I would be a loser. He was tall, he had sandy, curly hair. He had a twinkle in his eye and gave me a big hug.

We all decided to go to another dance place, and then Joan decided to go back to the bar. Ken and I danced till late.

"I'd like to see you next Friday again. We could meet at the Bombay Club."

I was up for it and agreed. Friday night came and I did not want to go in until I saw him in case, I was stood up. I saw him across the parking lot, and he was carrying a long-stemmed red rose.

We met and talked away the evening and wanted to see each other again. He was a realtor.

We made a date for the following Friday to go to a fish fry at his favorite bar. We got to the bar. He went to the restroom and the two men at the bar started talking to me.

Ken came back.

"You know it's not about us, it's about you. You have a presence."

I smiled.

He had recently been divorced, and one of the things he was missing was a microwave. I had an extra one and offered to bring it to his home. His wife evidently had taken most of the furniture. Was a big, beautiful house with barely anything in it. We talked into the late evening.

"You might as will stay over. It's so late for you to drive home."

He took me by the hand to his room. He had a huge king-size bed.

It had tons of all sizes of teddy bears all over it. To get in, I began to throw the teddy bears on the floor.

"Oh no, the teddy bears need to stay."

The following week he picked me up in his car; he had O'Doul's on the floor. I thought those were sodas. He was a total romantic, but after about six weeks, it was over for me. I discovered he was an alcoholic.

I inquired and found that alcoholics can drink O'Doul's all day, but it does keep enough alcohol in their system to keep them from getting the shakes. They can still pass an alcohol test. So much for Ken.

Chapter 23

ANOTHER ONE
BITES THE DUST

Sam and I still lived in the same building and we still cared about each other, we started going to dinner again. In a short time, Sam got a great job offer in Philadelphia and his daughter lived there; he decided to take the job. It was a great opportunity for him.

I flew to Philly a couple of times to see him. The last time, he picked me up at the airport, and when we got to his house, I opened my suitcase to show him something and there were all men's clothes. I had picked up the wrong luggage. He called the airport, and they had my luggage.

We had a great week, and he took me back to the airport. I stood in the line to check in and Sam had my small carry-on in his hand. He thought the girl at the counter, who had no clients would put him first. It was obvious she was not open. I stayed in the long line to wait. The man next to me seemed in a hurry and I had hours before my flight, I allowed him ahead of me.

Sam came back and shouted,

"Didn't you know that lady was ahead of you" and he hit him in the head with my hard case carry-on. That was the canary in the coal mine. The man had a straw hat on, I did not feel like he was hurt. I looked at Sam.

"Just leave" and he did.

The man shouted to me, "Tell your husband" I interrupted him.

"He is not my husband and you will never see me with him again."

When I got home Sam and I talked over the phone.

"I will never see you again."

"Never?"

"Never goodbye. "Several years later, I heard from our friends that he died of dementia.

By now the boutique, was very lucrative. There were now four girls running the store. One of my clients came to me one day and made an offer to purchase the boutique. There was a vacancy in the Pfister Hotel. She had always wanted to have a dress shop. She made me an offer I could not refuse. She told me if I agreed to sell, she was moving the dress shop a block away into the space at the Pfister Hotel. She felt she would have more traffic. She and I came to an agreement and I decided to go back to the furniture gallery, where I had previously worked. I had an interior design degree, and they had an opening. To be closer to work, I rented a condo until I could decide what I would do next. I stayed there a few years.

Chapter 24

MERCI

That fall, an eccentric looking man walked into the gallery and came near my desk. He had a brown bomber jacket on and a black beret. He was looking for a contemporary sofa. He reminded me of Anwar Sadat. I knew I did not have what he was looking for, but the conversation was enlightening.

"Are you from here?"

"Yes I am."

"I thought you might be from New York." Not finding what he was looking for, I walked him to the front desk and asked him to wait for me to go to my desk and get my card.

I walked over to my desk only to find him behind me.

"I need to see you again."

"Your name?"

"Jamal Robinson."

I smiled and he left. The next day I was called to the front desk for a floral delivery. I could not figure who would be sending me flowers. It was an unusual arrangement in a teal clear glass vase. The card read,

"Merci."

The following day Jamal called and asked me to go to brunch on Sunday at the Lakeside Café on the east side where he lived. I drove downtown in my new red Cougar. On my dream list was always a red sports car, which this was and to go to Paris. I had not accomplished that yet. I met him at the café. At lunch, I learned that he was Oriental, Brazilian and Black. He was from New York.

Going forward I saw him periodically, sometimes not for several months. Suddenly, he would appear. He would call at work and we would get together. After about six months he would call, and I picked up the phone.

"Oh, the dead live." He would laugh and we would meet.

He had been gone for several months out of sight. I knew he often flew to New York to see his family, but I had not seen him for a while.

I decided to buy two tickets to see Winton Marsalis at the PAC. The concert was six weeks away and in my mind Jamal and I would go together. I kept picturing it.

It was one week before the concert, and he did not surface. I was ready to ask a girlfriend to go with me. Enter Jamaal at the top of the stairs in the gallery.

"I have two tickets to go see Winton Marsalis."

I knew Jamaal was a total fan of jazz, especially Miles Davis.

"You are white witch."

"You want to go or not?" He did. He took me to dinner and then we went to the show. He again was leaving for out-of-town.

A few months later he came back, called me and I invited him over. He told me his father played piano at Radio City Music Hall in New York and he played piano as well. He played piano since he was four and played at the kinder concerts at Carnegie Hall.

I had a keyboard in my condo; one night when he came over, he sat and began to play. I myself took piano lessons, however never had the focus to practice much. I had thought he was jesting me; but when he put his fingers to the ivory and started with Autumn Leaves and continued to play without music for thirty minutes, I became a believer.

One balmy day he called. I really had missed his intrigue. He said he would be over about eight that evening. I left the garage door open and the door into the condo unlocked. I had can lights in every corner throughout for ambiance. I put on my black bra, black garter belt and my thigh high smokey hose with lace tops. I tossed on a long string of pearls. I played some Shirley Horn softly on my stereo. All my other lights were off. I slid into my bed with my long Nutria fur coat, to cover my sins.

It seemed forever; he came through the back door.

"Is anybody home?" No sound, he came around to the bedroom and burst out in laughter and threw open my fur coat. It was an interesting night, worth all my effort.

Didn't see him for several months and then he surfaced. It was a sunny afternoon and he sat in my living room, on my white pillowed sofa.

"Cat your genius is how you've decorated this place and your artwork."

All was well until something I said to him seriously upset him and he ranted and raved. He immediately stood up and I walked him to the door.

"C'est la vie."

"Do you know what that means?"

"Yep, that's life, goodbye."

Never heard from him after that. My friends and I would usually go to dinner on the weekends. We went to the theatre as often as possible, but my life still had something missing.

Chapter 25

WHAT COLOR ARE YOUR EYES?

I was busy these days working at the gallery and doing freelance writing for a small newspaper in the community. I was continuously writing poetry. I need to be constructive every minute in order to occupy my travelling mind. I really need to write a book, so I can live my fantasies, if my real life is not going to be fulfilled.

After a while I became restless with no new ideas in my life and nothing to fill my quiet moments. I decided to drive to see some of my friends in Madison, only an hour drive. We went to their hangout, with a bar, restaurant and a dance floor. I started going there each Friday night.

I met a group that my friends joined. I had always noticed a man, every time wearing a wide brimmed black hat. He hung with another crowd. My friends told me his name was Charles and that he was a filmmaker. I had been going there for quite some time.

One night, as he was passing, I asked, "Are you going to Sundance?"

"Yes, do you want to come along?" I laughed.

No more was said that night. A few weekends later I was leaving and at the end of the bar, the man with the hat, put his arm around me.

"How are you doing?"

"I'm leaving"

"I'm leaving too."

As we talked, he too was from Milwaukee, but this place was well known, he decided to start going there. When we got outdoors, he asked,

"Where are we going?"

"I'm going home." We stood and talked for quite some time, I guess I would say I talked. I was nervous.

"What color are your eyes?"

"Green."

I gave him my card. I had told him that I was a clairvoyant. I had been doing readings for years and he said that maybe he would get a reading.

He called and suggested he would like to come over and we could talk. I agreed. He came late and by that time, I thought he wasn't coming at all. I put on my long white silky gown. The doorbell rang. I threw on my robe.

"Sorry I'm late."

We talked for a while and I was nervous and told him, that I was dressed and then thought he was not coming so undressed. He wanted to take advantage.

"Not tonight."

We started seeing each other when he was free.

We started talking about his filmmaking. He had only one film he was working on for many years. He had a daughter that was born with some disabilities, that would continue all her life. He was entirely invested in making sure his daughter had as close to a normal life as possible, that that became his whole life.

He was a Professor at UWM Madison, in the art department to make a living to support his daughter. His wife and he had divorced. His life then became more complicated. His daughter ended up living with him because his former wife had a nervous breakdown.

I got the chance to meet Miriam. Charles had filmed her since birth.

She was beautiful and happy with her long dark hair. Her hair was always perfect. It was always tied back in a long ponytail with a big pink ribbon as she sat in her wheelchair. He loved her so much. She could not feed herself nor could she speak clearly.

I think I loved him for the beautiful father he was being. If she would get angry because she could not communicate easily, he would start singing, you are my sunshine, and she would then sing along and calm down.

Who would not love the man, that loved his daughter that much?

We could not see each other often because of Miriam's needs. If we did get together, he had to get a caregiver. When he did, he come over, the minute the door opened, he would grab me and kiss the daylights out of me and recite Robert Frost. How I waited for that, then go to bed and make love.

Was not the kind of relationship I was looking for, but it was beautiful and impossible to resist. He knew how to treat a woman. We saw each other on and off for about six years.

One day he came over and told me that he would be moving to Naples in Florida because the weather would be much better for Miriam. We drifted; he would call occasionally, but the relationship could be no longer. He said that we were each on a mission. He felt and I agreed that we had an Agape love. He still was making the film of the life of Miriam, and he was hell-bent on being in the Cannes film Festival. He was married to the movie.

I seemed to be doing more counseling than clairvoyant work these days. My clients appreciated the incite and left my home feeling enlightened. I was an excellent counselor as well. I thought that I was on a mission because of my gift. I agree with Charles; we each had a mission.

Each one of us had the same mantra. Be the one who makes a difference. I thought, be well my friend and successful in your mission. We lost contact.

I continued my counseling and Interior design work halfheartedly.

Chapter 26

LET'S DANCE

I had enough of Interior design and living near the Gallery. I looked and found a new apartment near the lake where I felt home. I left my job as money was no issue and decided to spend more time writing. I was sometimes writing four hours a day. I really wanted to get the book published, but never knew the story would be that easy. The editing is what would take the most time. To take a break, I would go to dinner with my friends. I needed some groceries; I stopped at the market to buy some fish. I wanted to start eating healthier. The butcher and I had a little small talk. We both seemed to chatter.

"I bet you like to dance."

"There are not many places in Milwaukee to dance."

"I'll show you." He turned over a hamburger carton and asked me to put my phone number on it.

I hesitated for a while, but I do like to dance. I finally gave him my card.

"I would just like to talk". He said we could get together at the food court in the shopping mall at 2 o'clock on Wednesday.

I got there first, and he came up the elevator, he looked fine. He had a great-looking striped shirt, sleeves rolled up, and great-looking trousers with a gait in his step. He had a full head of snow-white hair brushed back. We sat and talked. He asked,

"How old are you?"

"I can't believe you want to know."

"I asked because I need to tell you that I am quite a bit older than you. I have been retired for quite some time."

"What was your profession?"

"I was a commercial realtor." We got past the age conversation. He was ten years older than me.

At the end we did make a date to go dancing in the afternoon. He picked me up and wore a fine tan pin-stripe suit. I wore a black and white floral organza dress. When we got there all the old people were dressed casually. I found out he lived near me and often we would have dinner at his house. I brought something I cooked or sometimes he cooked. He would not go out to dinner because he knew what happened behind the scenes in a restaurant. He started to occasionally kiss me, I thought he was a vacuum cleaner. My lips hurt. It was no wonder he said his wife would say, "Must we do this again?" I certainly had to teach him a few things. He certainly did not know much about a woman.

After a couple of times, he invited me to his room. He wore hearing aids and one night, I was caressing his head and realized I had one of the hearing aids in my hand.

Not to spoil the moment, I carefully hung on to it until we went to the table and had a glass of wine.

At his age one only snuggled. Another evening he lost one of his hearing aids and couldn't find it anywhere. He got a flashlight and we looked everywhere and then we were both on our knees laughing and looking under the bed. We still did not find it. A moment later, he found it on the bathroom sink, where he left it.

After a short period of time, we didn't seem to have much in common, I decided to stop seeing him. I was thinking maybe my mother was right, "No man will ever please you."

Chapter 27

TIME TO TRAVEL

I purchased a new violin and began taking lessons. I played since I was eight and through high school, but never was that good. Practice is the key and I have no patience. I took three years of piano lessons. I often dusted my keyboard. I figured right now is a good time to keep myself occupied.

Mildred and I drifted over the years. She got more involved in her father's business. After her dad's retirement, Mildred was able to sell the business. Mildred shared with me that she hadn't seen her son Brad for several years. He was married to the military. He occasionally inquired how Jake, Marie and Ann were doing, but rarely. It made her sad to lose him to the military.

Becoming restless, I had to go to Paris to fulfill my dream. I wanted to go by myself so I could see everything that was important to me. I called my travel agent and booked the trip. I called Marie and Jake to let them know that my trip would be in fall. They were excited for me.

Saturday, the phone rang, and Marie explained to me through tears that they were trying to have another child. The doctor upon examining Jake, told him they would not be able to have more children. It was crushing to hear. Marie got pregnant so quickly, I never gave it a thought they would have a problem.

Early September I took my vacation, got the date set and flew to Paris. I checked in at the Hotel Lutetia. It is the only luxury Palace hotel on the Left Bank. Historically Picasso and Matisse stayed there. Josephine Baker was a regular. Its bar became a popular place for jazz. De Gaulle spent his honeymoon there.

I picked this hotel because it was within walking distance of the Luxembourg Gardens, the Musée d'Orsay and the Tuileries Garden. I would only be gone for ten days. I had to pick and choose.

I for sure wanted to see the Musée Rodin, and the Sacré Coeur. I could take the Metro also. It was an ambitious trip because I spoke little French and it was my first trip out of the country. I knew I would need to come back. The week went quickly, I didn't want to go back home ever. Reality set in and I flew back.

The next year the idea of living in Paris engulfed me. I kept in touch with Ann. She wanted to study in France. We shared the love of France. Ann shared that she was seeing a fellow named John and she was in love and they just got engaged. She had started seeing him several months ago. She felt sure he was the one. She was a fine artist and she loved to sew and create fashion. Marie sewed all Anne's clothes as a child.

I continued design work, and worked on my poetry book, Evolution of a Soul. It was a year with Paris was on my mind.

Chapter 28

MOVE TO PARIS

few things I knew, I still had a novel in me, and I wanted to live in Paris permanently. I talked to my family, and they encouraged me and said they would come to see me when I moved there. I have always made good decisions swiftly. This would be one of them

I had done a lot of research to pick my new home. I wanted my apartment near the Champs Élysée so I could enjoy the surroundings. I wanted to live in the eighth arrondissement. I finally sorted it all and found my new place. The apartment was on the seventh floor and had a lift. The address was 19 Rue de la Tremoille. It was a huge white building with balconies all along, with the red door at the entry. The living room and bedroom had windows across the wall. I need a lot of light.

In Paris you can purchase apartments. I bought it because I was not going back. Marie and Jake knew I was going to move, but when reality set in, they were sad to see me go.

It was a new experience to arrange the move, hoping to make the best decisions.

On my last day before moving, Marie flew in and we hugged and teary eyed we went to lunch.

My flight took off early Tuesday morning.

On arriving in Paris, I hailed a taxi at the airport. My head was spinning. Did I really do this? Yes, I did. The dream is now reality.

There was much to get used to, the language, as I know little French and getting around on the Metro. I didn't keep any furnishings as it cost so much to send anything abroad. I spent the first week buying furniture and furnishings.

Once settled, I got a job at the Parisien libéré, the morning paper as a freelance writer. I also filled in at a small boutique. I was born to travel and thanks to Mr. Lewis, everything was possible. I was in love with my decision to move to Paris. Every day was special.

Marie called, "Are you loving your new life? Ann and I were discussing that she would love to go see grandma."

"I would love to see Ann, when is she planning on coming?"

"She was thinking of coming next month and could only stay for a few weeks at the most." Marie put Ann on the phone.

"Well make your travel arrangements Ann. Let me know and I will be available to you. Is John coming with you?"

"No Grammy, just me. John needs to study for his master's degree."

Was a couple of weeks and Ann had already bought her ticket. She flew in on a Wednesday. I met her at the airport with hugs and kisses. It was great to see her; it had been too long. We went to all the cafés and did a ton of shopping and enjoyed each other's company.

We were sitting at the dining table having tea, and Ann noticed my ruby ring. I told her it had been my mother's and when she passed, it came to me.

"You like it so well Ann, when I pass, I will leave it to you."

"Oh, grandma don't talk about that."

We had a wonderful time together. The visit seemed short; it was time for her to leave. With hugs, kisses and tears, I sent her off. She was anxious to get back to John. The year was a whirlwind for me. I found several new friends. They were generous finding little cafés and small boutiques around Paris for us to enjoy.

Chapter 29

SPRING, NEWFOUND LOVE

*O*n a whim I popped in at a travel agency, knowing I wanted to travel Europe. I wanted to go on a tour because I would be traveling alone, and it would be easiest for me. I found a wonderful Trafalgar tour covering two countries or four, all of which I would love to see.

Spring seemed like a wonderful time to travel and I booked the trip. The stops were Germany, Switzerland and you could choose a continuing flight to Italy and France.I already lived in France, but two things I hadn't yet to see were Versailles and the Moulin Rouge. I decided on the four-country trip.

There was a limit to the size of the luggage one could take because we were traveling on buses sometimes and staying at several different hotels. You will place your luggage outside the room, and it will be loaded on the buses from hotel to hotel. The day came and I was ecstatic.

On the plane, I met a man named David who also was traveling alone. He was seated next to me. As we first began to talk, he told me he was from Rouen about an hour and a half from Paris. He was the CEO of an engineering firm back in Rouen. He had just retired. He sold the company to his two sons. We seemed to stick together because there were a lot of couples. We hit it off from the get-go. It seemed we knew each other forever. We shared so much, so soon.

He lived in Montmartre right now, and I lived in Paris, a lot in common. We both enjoyed fine art, we seemed to crave Italian food and both of us were constantly laughing. He had such a joy about him. He seemed like he loved the world. I thought he was a little naïve. He always wanted to make sure he didn't hurt anyone's feelings, and I believed he wanted to take care of the world and carry it on his shoulders.

David had recently left his wife; her name was Sondra. She still lived in Rouen.

"Oh, the home of Gustave Flaubert."

"Yes."

He commented that he needed a trip to think things through. He felt he had to leave home as he had done once before, and this time he really needed to look at how his life would unfold going forward.

We talked throughout the trip about his life with Sondra and how my life was with Henry. We had the same issues. Our spouses were each good people, but certainly didn't match.

It didn't bother me; we were only friends and he enjoyed taking care of me on this trip. If we were going up a steep hill, he would hold my hand. When we were getting into the buses, he let me go first. The more we talked, the more we laughed.

I couldn't help it, from the first day I met him I realized that he was complex and was a great conversationalist. I just fell in love.

I never was a believer of love at first sight, but there was something about him that warmed the cockles of my heart. He was a gentle soul and had such a beautiful spirit. "A heart beats because someone is loved." My heart was feeling full, I was careful about what I would say to him. I tended to say cute, sexual tidbits.

This time I felt it was for real and I didn't want to step over any lines. I just met him. It seemed as we traveled from city to city, we grew closer. His heart radiated love.

The first stop was Germany, and we all went to the cuckoo clock factory. I never saw that many clocks or heard so many different sounds. Cuckoo, cuckoo. The clocks all had beautiful wooden carvings. We took a boat trip on the Rhine. I never cared for German food, but I did love their bakery. Nothing like a great Apple strudel. I did speak German.

All our luggage was loaded for us on the bus. We traveled to Switzerland and there we took the red cog train straight up and I do mean straight up to the Swiss Alps.

He knew I was frightened. He held my hand and reassured me he was there for me. It was breathtaking far above the clouds. This is as close to heaven as I have ever been. We had a drink at the top and enjoyed the view. You could see a patch of blue, but mostly puffy white clouds that looked like cotton candy. It was amazing to be that high up. It was a spiritual experience. We stopped at a little shop to pick up some Swiss chocolate.

Some people on the tour were going home and others were continuing to Italy, including David. We flew out of Zurich to Rome.

I have always wanted to go to Italy. The fashion is fabulous there in the small little shops, and I love Italian food. It was close to my favorite part of the trip. The day we went to the Trevi fountain, it rained. He bought me an umbrella from one of the street vendors. We had to throw our three coins in the fountain. I turned my back to the fountain and threw my coins over my head into the fountain.

I was dreaming of us being together forever, so that's what I wished. I threw so hard, I almost fell in. Not to worry David caught me. We didn't climb the Spanish stairs because of the rain.

We strolled around, I noticed that there were masks everywhere, in every boutique. I knew I was going to buy one. It had to be the most beautiful, in my eyes. I was told that masks originally were created for medical reasons during the Bubonic plague. The mask I picked had a picture of Venice and a gondola.

We took a boat over to Burano to the Murano glass factory. It was totally amazing what the artisans could do with blowing on the heated glass. David and I sat on a bench and were impressed. They had a boutique to buy treasures. I couldn't resist this little blown glass giraffe. It was a golden clear glass with little black dots. Its legs were so fragile looking. I hoped it would get home safely.

Next day David and I went with the group to Venice and had to go on a gondola. You could hear the Venetian music in the distance, O Sole Mio. The gondolier explained the front of the boat. There is a comb with six teeth pointing forward, standing for the six districts of Venice. Between the six prongs indicate the three main islands of the city Murano, Burano and Forcillo. It didn't seem like a tour, it seemed like David and I were there alone.

He and I rode together, and it was such a romantic dream for me. He was always a gentleman. He sat with his arm around me for a picture. I never felt that he was completely into me. I felt he thought I was a wonderful person, but not a romantic interest. I couldn't help that I was in love with him. Love is a feeling, and feelings can't be wrong, they just are.

One can't go to Rome, without going to the Vatican so we did. The ceiling of Michelangelo was unimaginable. As we walked through the Vatican, David and I felt shallow because all this money was spent by the Catholic Church on the Vatican, and the general public was poor. There was marble and gold everywhere.

A portion of your taxes went to the Vatican, whether you were Catholic or not, or believed or did not. The last moments in Rome, we ate at the base of the Coliseum and drank French wine.

On a day trip to Florence, the city of statues, the most notable was the statue of David. It was seventeen feet tall.

We walked through the streets, stopped at the Piazza della Signoria, the most famous Square in Florence and fed the birds.

The next stop Paris. One of the side trips was Versailles. Neither David nor I had ever seen Versailles. I had been a Francophile and I loved the 1700s. For me it was super important to go to Versailles. I felt like it was a walk back in time. The outer gates were gold. Everything was ornate. All artworks had golden frames. Each room had beautiful period furniture. I had heard that Louis XIV had the flowers changed in the gardens daily to match the dresses of the maidens. The

Hall of Mirrors was breath taking. That's where the royalty danced till the wee hours of the morning. All the walls were mirrored. Many sparkling, crystal chandeliers hung from the ceilings and were reflected in the mirrored room. The gardens were all perfectly manicured. Time to go because that evening, our tour was going to the Moulin Rouge. What an awakening for me. Our tour arrived, huge red neon signs were flashing, Moulin Rouge. We entered and were seated right at the stage for dinner. The room was majestic. To look up and see tiers of round tables with little lamps with red pleated shades to create the ambience. The performance put me in mind of Las Vegas. The act that stands out in my mind was the gigantic blue lit ice cube rising from the floor, with a mermaid inside. How enchanted.

David and I sat together, as we were always together on the trip and he took my picture outside in front of the Moulin Rouge. In my mind I wanted to hug him and kiss him and hold his hand.

What a finale to a great trip. I never, never looked David in the eyes. I in the past, have looked someone in the eyes when I'm speaking with them. All the while I knew him, I never, never looked in his eyes. I feel the reason was, I loved him so much, and I didn't get the same feeling back. We were on the same spiritual page. That to me was important.

The tour seemed to end too quickly. David hugged me, told me what a great time he had and asked for my cell and said we could get together soon.

When I arrived back at my apartment, there were several messages on my answering machine. While I had been on the tour, Mildred's nephew, Josh was trying to reach me to tell me that Millie had passed. I guess he couldn't find my cell phone number until he called Marie. Brad was out on a mission and couldn't come either. Josh told me that Marie, Jake and Ann had flown in because they knew I wouldn't be able to come. They all hadn't seen each other in a while. Josh told me that Mary, Mildred's daughter was surprised how much her daughter and Ann looked alike. They could be sisters.

I had to sink into my chair. I was exhausted from the trip and my best friend ever would no longer be there for me. We had had many great times and laughed hard and cried a lot. It would take me a while to grieve and recover from my loss. I am called on to be the strong one again.

After the trip, David and I began to see each other on the weekends. I shared with him about my friend's passing.

"David, I need to tell you something. I love you as a person."

"I feel the same about you."

David, I am in love with you."

"I have known that. I'm not the one; I wish I could be."

"I promised myself to say this to release myself. I kind of thought that because I never thought of going to bed with you, and I never thought of making love with you. I just love you."

The next day, he called me and asked,

"Sooo, are you going to stop loving me?"

"No, I will always love you, my love is unconditional."

I never figured out why he asked the question, being he wasn't going to be with me anyway.

We continued to go to dinner on weekends to some of the finest restaurants in Paris and always had a beautiful time. He always insisted on paying. The glint in his eye, the gate in his step, and the beat of his heart, captured me. I never felt like this before in my life. I couldn't seem to control it, nor did I want to. I just loved him inside and out. I had always said I would marry a minister.

David had no church now, but he did have a church and was a minister when he lived in Rouen. I thought this was it. We had such a deep spiritual connection. A couple of weeks went by and we were having such a fine time. I was more in love than ever; I didn't feel it reciprocated. That is one thing about David, he never gave me any false hope.

The following week, David asked me to meet him at a café on the Champs-Élysées. I thought it was unusual because usually he picked me up. I told him I would get a ride. I figured that he would drive me back to my apartment. He suggested we meet at the Café Buci.

We ordered a drink and David looked a little nervous.

"Cat I have something to tell you. I have been talking to Sondra, and I have decided to go back to Rouen and make it work. I knew I wasn't everything that I should have been and now I'm going to try to be all that. She says that she has changed."

I could feel the tears in my heart.

"I will always love you; I love you so much that I want you to be happy. I love you that much."

He reached his hands across the table and took mine. "Let's pray."

He prayed that I would find the perfect person for me.

Chapter 30

Don't Tell God Your Plan

He did take me home. He was stone cold. I did love him enough that I wanted him to be happy, but I thought I could fill his needs. There were many things he told me about her, that I thought I would be a much better match. I guess it wasn't written that way. I pray for his happiness every day. I feel one day he again will have to leave. It may not be for me, but I feel he deserves better for himself.

I was sad and empty. I not only lost the love of my life, but I also lost a special friend. I'm a big girl, I can pick up the pieces and go on. I understand that if he did not feel that way that I cannot love enough for two. My emotional self-had to grieve.

Chapter 31

SURPRISE, SURPRISE

I had been told by a French man at the apartment building, that there was a special place I would enjoy lunch, the Café Cassette. When I arrived, I could see why he suggested I go there. There were yellow awnings all around the building. There was outdoor dining around the perimeters. At the archway to the entrance was a garland of pink, blue and yellow flowers. I went to sit at a small round table with two delicate wicker chairs. On each side there were tall vases with sprays of reeds about four feet tall and sporadic colored flowers. I was sitting in a little cove, having a cup of tea waiting for my order.

I noticed there were three servicemen sitting at a table near me. They were in uniform. They looked like high-ranking servicemen. One of them seemed to be staring at me, I kept looking away. At some point, I could see he was walking toward me and my table.

"I know it would be unreal, could you be a friend of my mother's, Mrs. Williamson?"

"Why do you ask?

"You look familiar to me like a mom of someone I used to date. I know it would be uncanny being here in Paris."

"What's your mother's name? "Mildred Anderson."

"I loved her; I am sorry for your loss."

"My daughter is married to Jake Anderson. Could you possibly be Brad Anderson?"

"Matter of fact I am. This is surreal, how is your daughter Marie? I used to date her, and I always loved her. I never could get over her. I dated many women, but none measured up to Marie.

I would like to call you and have lunch with you and talk more about this. I must go because the guys are waiting for me. I will call you if you would be so kind to give me your number."

"That would be very nice, and you may call me Cat."

He went back to his friends, I pondered. I always wished Marie and Brad would get married. He was such a fine young man and really adored Marie. It was Marie's life not mine. I had a croissant with crab meat and then I took a walk through this beautiful neighborhood. Everyone was enjoying their time in this park like area. I couldn't believe what just happened.

Brad called me and he suggested that we meet at Copenhague Paris at 1 o'clock Tuesday. I agreed and was anxious. He was right on time and suggested,

"Let's sit on the balcony, where it be a little quieter so we could converse."

"Marie and Jacob have one child named Ann. They would have liked more but were unable."

"My mom had sent me pictures of my cousin Jake and his family."

"Will you be in the city for a while?"

"Yes, we will be here several months at least."

"I would like to invite you and your two friends, if they are available, for dinner at my home, a week from Saturday."

"If my schedule allows.I will call you."

Brad called and confirmed that the three of them could come.

"Dinner will be at eight."

I was thrilled to have dinner guests. I enjoyed cooking and I am into presentation. I decided to have Cornish hens, wild rice, orange sauce and asparagus. Brad had mentioned that he would bring the wine. I wanted a light dessert, that would be Tiramisu.

Years back, I had enjoyed having Brad over for dinner and I thought he was always a fine gentleman. Marie had different ideas.

It was a delightful evening at dinner, but Brad and I didn't get much chance to talk about families.

I suggested as Brad left, that we might meet the next week at a café or my place and talk more about our families. I still couldn't get over that we would meet halfway across the world. It's highly unlikely to happen, but it did.

The following Wednesday, I called Brad and suggested we meet on Friday evening at Café Buci as I had been there before and enjoyed it. He agreed we would meet at 7. I arrived first.

Brad was always late, but that night, he was on time. He suggested we eat in an alcove where it would be quiet. There were cane legged tables and chairs. Quite charming. We ordered wine.

"I was on a tour in Europe when your mother passed."

Brad and I talked a lot about Millie and Marie.

"I did go through some depression when I got the letter from Marie."

We talked a lot, especially about his mom and the memories.

I invited him over the following week to show him all the pictures I had of Ann, Jake's daughter, being Jake was his cousin. I as a grandmother, was proud of Ann as she had grown up to be such a fine young lady. I had all the pictures in an album from the time she was a baby. Ann would be my only grandchild.

Brad seemed more than interested. He had seen some of them as his mother tried to keep him updated of family matters. Ann looked more like Brad than Jake and I somehow had always wondered, if possibly just possibly, Brad could be the father.

Who am I the one to say, I always kept quiet. Jake has been the best father for Ann and loved her so much.

When Brad was looking at the album, it seemed he looked so long at each picture and it appeared his eyes were a bit watery. I had dinner ready and we had such a nice time and I enjoy Brad. I always did. He had such a genuinely good spirit as he still does. It was a lovely evening and Brad said he needed to make it an early night.

A week went by and Brad called me.

"Cat would you mind if I stopped over sometime this week, for a little while. I'd like to talk to you about something."

"I must work at the paper on Wednesday. How about Thursday evening about eight? I will cook us a little something and we can share a glass of wine."

Thursday couldn't arrive soon enough because I could tell Brad had something heavy on his heart. Brad came in the door, carrying a bottle of Sauvignon Blanc. I thought he had a different look on his face. He generally was such a happy soul, but tonight was different. I made some Cordon Bleu, candied carrots and brown rice. He was complementary about my cooking. After dinner I suggested,

"Let's go to the living room and sit on some comfortable chairs with our wine."

Brad wanted to talk about Jake and Marie. I already knew where he was going with this conversation. I didn't yet know what I was going to say.

"Brad, tell me what's really on your mind."

"Cat, I don't know how to say it, because I care about you and I care about your family, you have always known that. I heard through my mom, how quickly Marie and Jake had the first baby. I don't know how to tell you, but Marie did not want to make love with me the night before I left for the Air Force, but I admit I was the one who convinced her. That is the only time, I want you to know, that she was willing to make love with me."

"I think I know what you're trying to suggest. How can you be sure?"

"Now that I've seen all the pictures, I feel more convinced than ever. Josh, my cousin and I started hanging together a lot, right before Mary's wedding. In one of our conversations, he told me that he and Jake had had rheumatic fever as kids and the doctor, when he examined Jake, told him he probably would never have children because Jake had a more serious case than Josh. I need you to make a promise to me that this conversation always, I repeat always stays between you and me until we die. Cat, I need to beg you for one last thing. I would like you to place pictures of me that you could print from my cell, to put in the album until you pass. Ann will have the memory of me. I know Jake, to Ann, is her father and he loves her so much, and Marie loves him. I would never want Ann to be hurt, but I feel this is something that is part of her life."

I hung my head. Wow, oh wow, what a concept. Could this possibly be? I kind of thought this all along myself.

Brad poured us just one more glass of wine and we each had to think this through.

"I am not in total disagreement with you, but this is a lot to think about. I would like to have you come over again next week, I know time is getting short before you have to leave with your unit."

"The only thing is, I am leaving next Saturday for a reunion with some of the guys from my last unit."

"Alright, let's meet before that." We decided to meet the following Friday at seven. We agreed it should be at my house.

"I will bring dinner."

There was a lot to mull over for both of us.

Friday came and with a lot of thought, Brad was more than likely right. The idea that only he and I would ever know this until I passed, would be a considerably good idea.

My thinking, Jake and Marie were happy, and Ann loved her dad. When Brad came, we spent the evening until late putting his pictures in the order he wanted in the album. After he left, I was wearing out from the whole idea as I knew he was also.

He was leaving on Tuesday for the reunion with his buddies. He was flying out to New York, traveling on Air France. Brad would be gone for a little over a week. I invited him for dinner when he came back to hear all about the trip.

Tuesday Brad flew out. Shortly after five o'clock, I rushed to my TV. The program was interrupted with Breaking News, Air France flight 4595, a Concorde supersonic airplane crashed in a suburb of Paris today, July 25. The airplane went down in flames almost immediately after takeoff killing all 109 people on board and four others on the ground.

That was Brad's flight.

Only one week before, I had hired my housekeeper Eleanor and she happened to be there on Tuesdays. Good thing she was there, I passed out on the floor, they tell me. She happened to be in the kitchen and came running. She sat me in a chair, put a cool cloth on my forehead.

"Just breathe."

She could not calm me. There was no solace. I always have felt so alone. I feel, who am I on this island of life? It has been my question, my entire life, more now than ever. This just couldn't be, couldn't be.

Chapter 32

ELEANOR

After this tragedy I didn't care to live alone. A friend of mine Marguerite, in the next apartment knowing how I felt, had referred Eleanor. She knew Eleanor was looking for permanent work. She had no family left; years ago, both her parents died in Germany and her husband recently died. They had no money, she needed to work. My neighbor had known her for a long time. She's a wonderful lady with that adorable German accent.

The next week I called Eleanor.

"I would enjoy you considering living with me permanently. If it would work for you, that might be a resolution for both of us. Give it some thought and call me tomorrow."

Eleanor called me and said she decided she would like to move in with me.

We hit it off from the first day. She was efficient, loving, caring. I cherished her. After Brad's death, I never seemed to be enthused about anything. Eleanor gave me that needed companionship. She was a little stout. She would walk from side to side with her heavy shoes on. She liked to wear an apron over her dress. She wore her salt-and-pepper hair back in a pug. Sometimes we would speak German, as I know the language well. I took the language in high school; it stuck and to this day. I speak it fluently. I no longer worked, a little as a freelance writer and I was working on what I thought would be my final book.

Eleanor and I would spend a lot of the evenings sharing our stories. She talked about her life in Germany and I talked about Marie, Jake and Ann.

"Eleanor you must've heard my whole life story by now."

Eleanor and her husband never had any children, she loved to hear the stories about Ann that Marie often told me.

Eleanor lived with me for a while and then one day I told her the ultimate story. The story was about the album. I told her she was the only one on earth beside Brad and me that I would share the album with, as I promised. I kept the newspaper article that had the plane crash in it.

After some time, I needed to keep my mind off the crash, and it hurt my heart that Ann would never get to meet Brad. Life is not always fair, and things rarely go as you planned. Eleanor was my kind of lady. She had enough tragedy in her life, she knew how to be strong.

It took me a couple of years but, my book was ready for the editor and then for the publisher. I always wrote of events I could only dream of living. If I can't live the life that fits me, I will live it through my books. I don't know what publisher yet.

I know this book will be my finest hour. I have a few articles left that I'm doing for the paper as I promised, I think it's time for a glass of wine and then I'll go to bed and get some serious rest.

I think this was the best time of Eleanor's life and I enjoyed her company. Some of the things she told me, I would be able to use in my new book. We would talk to the wee hours of the night and realize; the morning would come quickly.

Neither of us had real jobs right now, we could sleep in. Eleanor made the best strudel and coffee cakes; I was gaining a little weight. One thing about German desserts, they are near perfect and delicious. I never cared much for German food, but Eleanor's desserts were best bar none.

One night after Eleanor went to bed, I remembered Brad's crash. I went to my desk drawer and pulled out the newspaper article, settled in my favorite reading chair. I couldn't believe that that ever happened. My eyes were tearing up and I realized I was getting sleepy, took off my glasses and laid them on the table with the paper.

Next day, Catherine's neighbor Marguerite came running over. "What's going on Eleanor?"

"I woke up early this morning and went to the kitchen to put the tea on and then bring it to Catherine. I saw Catherine in her chair, but Catherine was slouched over. I soon realized that Catherine was not moving. I called the authorities, and they came quickly, but they could not revive Catherine. They told me she had passed; they had done their best."

I took care of that as best as I could and then looked for the phone number for Marie. It was an awful call. I had to repeat myself a couple of times for Marie to believe me. I was as devastated as Marie. Marie dropped the phone, and her husband came on, and I explained to him what happened."

The following day Marie and I talked about the details. Catherine would be cremated. I made the plans for the day following Marie and Ann's arrival.

Jake could not come, due to his work. John was teaching. Marie and Ann flew to Paris. I greeted them at the door,

"Come in."

They all hugged amongst the tears.

"Come in the living room. I will bring tea and some croissants."

No one wanted to leave the apartment.

Marie and Ann looked around the apartment and Eleanor showed them the chair that Catherine had died in, they looked at the round table next to the chair; on it were lying Catherine's glasses, and a newspaper.

Eleanor was hesitant to talk about the newspaper.

Marie nor Ann mentioned the paper. They were too distraught. Marie and Ann did not know about Brad. I became sick to my stomach to think that I will have to be the one that tells Catherine's and Brad's story.

The next day, we held the service and went back to the apartment. We did have to get into Catherine's things and decide to empty the apartment. I would have to have a new place to live.

On opening Catherine's closet, Ann noticed something special.

"Look mom, isn't this beautiful?

It was a robe, in a clear plastic hanging bag. Ann unzipped the bag and admired it. It was a coral-colored long robe with a tan satin lining and a tan satin hood. It had coral-colored ropes to tie it. At the end of the sleeves, it had a wide band of tan satin. The gown was tan satin with tan lace across the bust.

"Look, it still has tags on it. I guess it has never been worn. It's so beautiful. I wonder why."

Eleanor walked into the room in that moment.

"Catherine bought that for her French wedding night. She had told me that she would not wear it until that happened.

On the floor of the closet were two elegant pairs of slippers. They were both satin, both pair were backless spikes. The ivory pair had ivory marabou across the toes. The black pair had black marabou across the toes.

Marie and Ann were astonished by what they found. They were speechless as they stared at each other.

No one or at least very few would have known this side of Catherine. Catherine was always known in wide circles as a classy lady. She was eloquent in her speech, cherished by almost everyone. She was generally a conservative author, artist and counselor.

Marie and Ann looked around the bedroom and wondered, now what might be in the chest of drawers. Marie opened the top drawer.

"Oh!"

"Mom what did you find?"

"I guess I didn't know my mom."

Marie held up a black garter belt, a red garter belt, thigh-high black hose with lace around the top.

In the next drawer, Marie found lacey sets of bras and panties in red with white lace edges, black with white lace edges, purple, and many other colors, all sets. Marie opened the third drawer and there were several red and black sets of lingerie.

"You know mom we opened every drawer except the bottom drawer."

When they opened that drawer, it seemed unusual, no clothes, an album marked Ann and a small box.

Next to it, an envelope marked Marie. They both sat on the floor cross legged. Marie grabbed the envelope and tore it open. Ann wanted to see what was in her mother's envelope.

Marie couldn't quite figure it out, but there was some paperwork in it from an attorney. It said, Ms. Catherine Woods, Mr. William G Winters has left the city. We cannot locate him for support of Marie Catherine Woods. There still in the envelope was a picture.

Marie knew it was the picture of her biological father. Marie and Ann were so involved in Marie's letter, that they had not yet got to look at the album.

First, Ann was curious to open the little box. She opened it and the tears streamed down her face.

"Grandma had always told me that someday I would get her Ruby ring."

Ann put the ring on and wouldn't you know it fit perfect.

The album was marked Ann; they were anxious to look at the album.

As they sat and opened the album, there were all the pictures of Ann, that Marie had sent over the years. How sweet, they thought. The last pages of the album had pictures, many military pictures of whom?

At first Marie didn't catch on because she had not seen Brad for many years. He looked so different and how likely would it be that he was in Paris.

As they continued to look through the album, the last picture was of Brad and Marie when they were dating. Marie and Ann looked at each other in wonderment. Something was going on. Ann had no clue, but she did have things in the back of her mind.

Eleanor came in the room with tea.

"Before we do anything more, she suggested, let's have tea. There are some things that I feel Catherine would want me to tell you. She was in a café one day on the Champs and as uncanny as it is, Brad was in Paris and recognized Catherine. They decided to get together and talk about their families. The rest is history. Now you girls go and check out the album."

Marie was starting to think back. She, in her mind was remembering that night before Brad left. She also was thinking that Ann came two months early.

"Oh my God!" It hit Marie. What could I tell Ann or Jake if Brad is the father? The truth is Jake and I had already talked through the possibility years ago.

"Ann, your father and I had this discussion. He already wondered, when you came early, but he loved us both and he and I just decided to raise you as our own, knowing there was a great possibility Brad was your biological father. I loved Jake, your father so much and he loved me that we agreed, Ann is our daughter.

What value would there have been at this point to deny our love for each other and our love for you."

Eleanor entered the room,

"I don't want to bother you, but is there anything you need? You both look so distressed understandably, but I am here for you, if there's anything I can do for you."

There were no words. All three of us were adjusting to the reality.

The next morning, no one had slept. Everyone was so restless for different reasons. Ann wanted to look at the album again, not understanding completely. Ann again opened the album; an envelope fell out. It was a letter that Brad had written to Ann.

Eleanor was right in the other room and saw the envelope fall out. She was trying to stay out of the fray.

Eleanor knew what was coming because Catherine had told her the whole story.

"Ann, before you open this envelope, could we sit, all sit around the table for a bit?

Catherine has left the entire legacy with me. I want to say, everything Catherine ever did was coming from love. She hopes you will still love her, when all this is said and done."

Marie had a lot to digest. First, would Ann still love her and would Jake want to leave her after all this. Ann didn't seem as shaken as Marie.

Ann always had questions about her genealogy, but she loved Jake so much, it really didn't matter much to her. She was anxious to open the letter.

Marie begged,

"Read it out loud. Eleanor and I will want to hear too."

"I don't know if I want to do that mom. I don't know what it will say or who wrote it. I may need some tissues to get through it. If you insist, I'll try."

Dear Ann,

I have always had you in my heart from the first pictures my mother sent me of you. I could see many features of you in me. I loved your mother from the first day I met her.

I will always love her more than any other woman. She is a wonderful person, but she did know her heart. I hope you will always follow your heart. I know what a great father Jake is to you.

I never wanted to interfere with the beautiful life your mom, Jake and you have created. I may not have been able to be a part of your life, but I always want to be part of your heart. I have loved you as my own.

We may never know, you and I, if I am your real father, but know that Jake and I love you equally. Jake may never have had any children, but you gave him your soul. What a great gift you are to your grandmother, your mother and Jake. I will forever be thankful that I have been able in some way to share your life. Know whether I am with you or away from you, you will be forever in my heart. All my love, Your Most Ardent Supporter.

There wasn't a dry eye in the room. All three of us, needed a tissue, maybe a box. All Ann could say is,

"How beautiful."

We all three agreed, there just can't be any more. There was more. Eleanor was told by Catherine to send the newspaper of the plane crash with the family.

Eleanor said,

"Do you see over on the table, that newspaper? Catherine brought it out from her desk drawer last night and was rereading it."

Marie and Ann had not noticed the paper, nor had they heard of the accident.

"How oh how for me to tell you. Brad was going to a reunion in New York to meet with his service buddies. Right after takeoff, the plane caught fire, and everyone was killed."

This was too much for everybody. Surprising that all three of us did not faint. All three of us were sick at heart. It was way too much for any one of us to absorb. The room was silent.

Marie and Ann had to leave the next day for Connecticut. The trip was long. Marie and Ann slept most of the way home.

Marie and Ann arrived back in Groton and Jake met them at the airport.

Marie called Eleanor.

"We are home safe."

Eleanor responded,

"Wonderful, I got a call today. This daughter lives in another city and her father needs a live-in caregiver. It is a mansion on the French countryside. I spoke with him and it appears he is a kind old gentleman and so well versed. It seems to be a good fit for me I need to let them know tomorrow."

The Anderson house was often silent. Everyone had their own thoughts. A week later, Ann didn't feel well. She thought it was all the events in Paris. The next week she felt no better and went to the doctor.

"Are you in a relationship right now?

"Yes, we are getting married in June."

"Oh! I need to tell you; you are going to be a mother."

Ann was silent.

Ann got home and told John. They were both surprised.

"Ann, maybe we should move the wedding, so you can fit into your dress. I love you, so now I love two of you."

CPSIA information can be obtained
at www.ICGtesting.com
Printed in the USA
FSHW011720070421
80223FS